THE LATTER DAYS

THE LATTER DAYS

Monte Dutton

CITIOFBOOKS, INC.
3736 Eubank NE Suite A1
Albuquerque, NM 87111-3579
www.citiofbooks.com
Hotline: 1 (877) 389-2759
Fax: 1 (505) 930-7244

Ordering Information:
Quantity Sales. Special discounts are available on quantity purchases by corporations, associations, and others. For details, contact the publisher at the address above.

Printed in the United States of America.

ISBN-13   Paperback   978-1-959682-17-2
                 eBook   978-1-959682-18-9

Library of Congress Control Number: 2022919510

Table Of Contents

CHAPTER 1
Up and at 'Em

Quite often, what I first realize when I awaken is how old I am. In the fog of gathering consciousness, it seems unbelievable. I count up the years. What year I was born. What year I was drafted. What year I made the All-Star Team. The two different years I got divorced. The year I was fired. It all adds up, damn it.

My left thumb hurts. I guess I slept on it wrong. I stretch it and test the range of motion that stops shy of causing it to throb. Then I rest it on the bookshelf next to the bed. It still hurts a little. I shuffle into the kitchen and put on some coffee. I take my morning meds and put my evening meds in a little container. I trundle to the bathroom because nature always calls at about the time my nose catches the scent of the coffee. I've concluded that bowel movements are about half psychosomatic. I return to the kitchen and stir the coffee. I turn on the TV, sit down, and watch a *Columbo* rerun. I plug in the phone, which has been left on overnight. I pick up the little appointment book. This is the Tuesday I have to go look at this high school kid who supposedly might be a first-round draft pick. The Portland Loggers don't pay me a salary anymore. They used to call what I am now "a bird dog." I sniff out a bird, and, if the Loggers shoot him, or sign him, it earns me a paycheck. Occasional paychecks for scouting, my pension, and appearances at autograph shows are about all I've got left to get by on. It's another reason I count the years. I can't believe how much money I used to have and how little I've got now. I'm doing all right. I make enough to pay my bills. The house is paid for. If I need something, I pay cash.

The day figures to be just another one full of "didn't you used to be Clyde Kinlaws?" If somebody down in – what is it? Vosbrinck? – asks me if I'd like to go have a beer somewhere, I'll do it. I like to drink, but I don't like drinking alone. It's too depressing. Even though I'm five years removed from being the manager of the Loggers, I still get my share of free beer.

Too damned many high school ballfields have lights these days. That means when some local rube wants to have a beer, it's usually just a beer. Then maybe there's a good-looking woman who's already drunk by the time I get there, and she hears who I am and thinks mistakenly that I've got money, well, maybe she takes me home, and maybe I get laid, and maybe she's divorced, and if I'm lucky and she doesn't still have a husband who works through the night, the sex won't require much commitment, and I'll have another place to crash next time I'm in the area. It's been a long time since I busted up an unhappy home. They tell me this life was a lot less treacherous back before all the cotton mills shut down, and most husbands stopped having a third shift to work on.

The hound-dog life ain't no good life, but, damn it to hell, all too often, it's my life.

As it turns out, the visiting team is Vosbrinck. The home team is Haldeman, which is a lakeside town just off Interstate 26, less than an hour's drive, and the hotshot prospect is from an affluent family, and he doesn't play anything but baseball year-around, and I can tell before I ever look at him that he's got a store-bought swing and a private coach with whom he studies video. He never even lays down a bunt during batting practice, and if his poor high school coach ever gave him a sign to do so during a game, the boy's dad would get him fired by the end of the month. I know the type. The type is everywhere. He lifts weights and takes supplements, and he can hit a high school fastball four hundred feet. He drives a four-wheel-drive Toyota pickup he got the day he got his license, and he enjoys hunting and fishing with all the sycophants who worship him and follow him around. He rules his roost better than any Rhode Island Red.

Let me look at my paperwork. His name is Ryne Standback, and he was named after Ryne Sandberg because his mom and dad grew up in Rockford, Illinois. I always liked Sandberg when I played against him, so the phenom has that going for him. He's a first baseman who throws right and switch-hits. He hits more home runs left-handed, but that's probably just because he sees more right-handed pitching. My dossier has all sorts of charts and graphs in it, some of which I understand, and a bunch of unexplained statistical acronyms and alphabetisms. It's funny that I know the difference between one and the other -- an acronym has to be read as a word on its own, like NASA -- but don't know the meanings of all the actual terms.

Ryne Standback has one hell of a MOKWOQ, though, whatever that is.

I'm a thoroughly intangible scout in a world grown full of tangibles. I got myself three sharpened No. 2 pencils, a stopwatch, a scorebook, a notepad, and the skills to analyze what my eyes can see. I've got a JUGS gun I never use unless I'm personally working out a pitcher. With this kid on display, all I've got to do is sit a row behind other scouts. A row of radars will be on display should I care to assess the oncoming heaters.

I finish my coffee and watch the Smithsonian Channel for a while so I know all about Idaho from the air. About halfway through, I get up and fix a breakfast of country ham and egg on buttered English muffins. I put the plate on top of the table. I roll up to my easy chair, which is going to require replacement sometime soon, and learn about Shoshone Falls and the Frank Church River of No Return Wilderness Area. Then I make myself presentable and head uptown without any plans other than to drop by one of my hangouts, the local office supply, where I can catch up on the gossip and buy a handful of rollerball pens from the dollar barrel.

Vern Crosley's opening remark is predictable.

"How was spring training, Clyde?"

I sat down in one of the comfortable office chairs that can be rolled around to facilitate discussion groups of several sizes and say, "Aw, I been back for about a week. My back's just now recovering from too many fungoes. Same old thing. Saw some old friends. Played a little golf. Acted like I know what I was doing to a bunch of prospects. Went out drinking one night with several teammates from twenty years ago. It's about the same every year. Two weeks and I'm ready to come home."

"What's the scuttlebutt?" Vern asks.

"I like the new manager, Gary Sjakich," I say. "He coached third base for me the last year I managed. At Triple-A last year, he won twenty more games than the big club. Knows the personnel. I expect the Loggers will do better, but you never know with these ballplayers today. I was impressed with the new third baseman, Jesus Hidalgo. He comes to camp in really good shape. They say he looked really good playing winter ball in the Dominican. The number two starter, Javon McRea, looks like he's put on fifteen or twenty pounds. I doubt that's a good thing."

Dub Whatley, who coached me in high school, asks me if I'm up for a round of golf this afternoon. He's about my speed. He's probably closing in on seventy, but, apparently, he plays every damned day.

"Nah, Dub, I'd love to play, but I gotta go scout a kid in Haldeman."

"Must be that Standback kid," he says.

"Yep. The club tells me he's likely to be a first- or second-rounder. I hope I can find somebody else who might make a low-rounder or a free-agent signing. The big-name prospects got so many people looking at 'em. Ain't enough scouting bonus money to go around."

"Who's Haldeman playing?" Dub asks.

"Vosbrinck."

"I can't remember the last big-time player come from down there," Dub says. "They had a right good football team last fall, though."

"I hope there's a good athlete with some raw tools," I say. "There won't be no secrets on that Haldeman roster. Standback's seen so many scouts, they probably took a good look already at any other prospect on the roster. It's my understanding Haldeman's got a couple who might get some money to play at small colleges, but not nobody who's ready for the pros."

Vern gets back from sending a fax to the woman from the jewelry store across the street. He just listens. Vern's not that interested in prospects. He wants inside dope on big leaguers. Sometimes I make something up, just so he'll have a little gossip to spread around town.

"I'd love to see that Standback kid play," Dub says.

"Well, you want to ride with me down there?" I ask.

"Nah, I can't do it today," he says. "I gotta leave here in a few minutes. Me and Lawyer Daggett s'posed to go off at two-thirty at River Falls."

I tell him to hit 'em straight.

"I'm about to order some lunch from the snack bar," Vern says. "Want a couple of hot dogs?"

I tell him I had a good breakfast, and I'm not in the habit of eating lunch these days. Dub gets up and starts working his way out the door. The bull session is about played out. I pay Vern for six blue pens and tell him to let me know the next time he's got some padded manila envelopes on sale. I decide I'll drive on down to Haldeman and knock around town a little. I might be able to find something out about the Standback kid mingling with the locals. High school coaches are unreliable. They promote their kids and don't tell you the dirt, like if the kid's selling weed on the side or knocked up his girlfriend. It's a long shot, but it helps sometimes that I've still got a mild, lingering celebrity, and baseball fans recognize me and want to come up and chitchat. Sometimes it's a pain in the ass, but it's never a bad idea to talk to folks and make them feel like they're important.

It's a lovely day for early March and all the more reason I wish this high school game was being played in the afternoon sunshine. It'll be cold tonight. I'm wearing jeans and a flannel shirt over a long-sleeved tee, but I've got two jackets, one light and one heavy, behind the seat of the pickup. It was Dub Whatley who got me in the habit of being excessively punctual. It doesn't matter whether it's a high school baseball game or meeting an old friend for supper. I take my time and get there early. Most of my friends are fashionably late. I'm annoyingly early. Haldeman's a nice little town. I look around for a while and settle on a coffee shop near a Food Lion and a Domino's Pizza. I order a banana-nut muffin and a large coffee, black with Sweet 'n' Low, and bide my time reading a spy novel on my cell. A fellow who looks as if he might be the village eccentric walks over and says I look familiar. I tell him I don't live here, but he sits down with his espresso. He's wearing a black-and-white-plaid, buttoned-down cap that makes him look mildly English. Lake Murray isn't far away. I bet he owns a sailboat.

"I got it," he says. "You used to play baseball."

I smile and wash down a bit of the muffin with coffee.

"Howdy," I say. "Name's Clyde Kinlaw."

"What brings you to our fair city?" he asks. "As I recall, you're from somewhere in the Upstate."

"Youngville," I say. "Born and raised. Finally moved back there. I'm scouting a kid at Haldeman High School."

"Ryne Standback," he says. "I was teaching him English about two hours ago."

"Decent kid?"

"Smart," he says. "A bit on the self-absorbed side, but that runs in star athletes."

"What's your name?" I ask. He says, William Sturges.

"I bet don't nobody call you Willie," I say.

"Will. Nice to meet you."

"My pleasure."

"I take it the Standback kid's a decent student," I say. "Is he likely to make a choice between college and signing a pro contract?"

"He committed to the Gamecocks," Will says, "but my guess is he's just using it for leverage."

"That's fairly common for a kid who's projected to be chosen in the first two, three rounds," I say.

"Not the first round?"

"I haven't seen him," I reply. "I've got a file the big club sent me. I'd say he's got a shot at the first round."

"Who do you work for?"

"The Portland Loggers," I say.

"You were their manager, right?"

"Yep. Five years ago," I say. "They let me go at the end of thirteen. I just do a little scouting on the side now."

"I'm a Boston fan," Will says. "You were with the Sox for a while, right?"

"I finished up with them. I enjoyed my half a season there. I was mainly a lefthanded pinch-hitter. By then, my knees were shot."

It seems like English teachers are always Red Sox fans.

"Ryne is a privileged kid," Will says. "His father owns a Kia dealership. His uncle's a lawyer. He's certainly a fine athlete, and I expect that means he works at it. He doesn't work much in English. My guess is he might be prone to let his ego get in the way."

"Everybody has a hard time when he has to compete against kids who got as much talent as he has," I say. "I certainly did, way back when. There's no way of knowing whether or not a kid can rise to the occasion. Hell, Will, he's a kid. He thinks he's grown up. He thinks he knows it all. Playing at the next level will either teach him some lessons or eat him alive."

"Between me and you, Clyde, I'd bet on the latter."

"Well, that's good to know," I say. "I'll take it under advisement."

"I better run along," Will says. "Maybe I'll see you at the game."

"I'll be there," I say.

CHAPTER 2
Just Add Water

━━◦═◦━━

$\mathcal{I}$t seems as if my days are seldom mediocre. If I kept a chart, I suppose the results would be inconclusive. Maybe I remember the splendid and wretched more than the uneventful. It's always seemed that way, though. As a player, I was forever streaking or slumping. I hardly ever went one for four with a sacrifice fly. Either I drove in six, or I didn't drive in any.

Everything went perfect in Haldeman.

The baseball field has a set of stands behind the dugouts. They're decent seats for the fans but of little use to scouts. Behind the plate is a gradual bank rising to a press box. I go back to the truck and get the fold-out, a canvas-covered chair I keep for just such an occasion. I sit it up about halfway up the bank. The other scouts crowd into the press box, there to share their insights and be mildly indoctrinated by the public-address announcer and the scoreboard operator. I get to keep to myself. None of the young scouts has much use of my opinion. They probably call me "Pops" when I'm not around. I'm as much a critic of theirs as they are of mine. They're winning, though.

I walk down to the dugouts and copy the lineups in my scorebook. The other scouts can get them in the press box, and they all use these little computers called "tablets." I still like doing it the way my daddy taught me. I just walk through the gate and see if there's a scorecard taped to the dugout wall. I don't announce myself. If someone happens to wonder who in hell I am, then I'll introduce myself as a scout, and if he asks "who for?" I'll say the Loggers. If he recognizes me as a player, I'll say "yeah, I had a few good years" and try to create the image

9

that I'm not wild about talking about it, but people seldom pick up on my hints, and I'll be gracious and maybe even tell one of the short tales I keep filed away. I've never had much taste for self-promotion. I don't volunteer anything, except, maybe, when somebody buys me a beer.

The Vosbrinck coach doesn't recognize me. He looks familiar, though. After a few awkward seconds, I realize he looks like Lionel on *All in the Family*. I liked Lionel. I make conversation for that reason alone.

"Coach, I'm Clyde Kinlaw," I saw. "I'm a scout. I came down here to look at this Standback kid from Haldeman, but is there anybody on your club I ought to look at?"

For some reason, Lionel doesn't tell me his real name. He sort of looks away.

"Kid playing catcher is as good an athlete is there is in this state," he says.

I look at my scorebook. "Wattson," I say. "Two T's."

"Taiquon Wattson," Lionel says. "Option quarterback in football. Shooting guard in basketball. Catcher for me. He's good at all three of them."

"I hope you don't mind me asking," I say, "but him being such a great athlete, why do you play him at catcher? Why not shortstop? Or center field?"

Lionel surveys the handful of others within earshot: a student trainer, a couple of scrubs in uniform, dugout scorekeeper.

"Talk to me after the game when ain't nobody around," Lionel says. "I'll tell you then."

I'm feeling a bit confused as I walk across the diamond to the Haldeman dugout. Why would he be reluctant to tell me why this kid plays catcher? Oh, well. Lionel is a man of mystery. This could not be said about the coach of the home-standing Haldeman Eagles. The guy is all over me by the time I reach the on-deck circle. Big fan of mine. We take a selfie. I sign a ball. Ryne Standback is a super young man, from a super family, has a super attitude, and he's right with God. I want to ask the salesman just exactly what is his bottom line on how much I've got to pay for the low-mileage, one-owner Camry that happens to play first base on Tuesdays and Fridays.

I tell him I'll see him after the game. I walk back to my chair not knowing his name, either.

Haldeman has won its first five games. Vosbrinck is three and one. Haldeman is in Class 4A and Vosbrinck 2A, which I can only assume means Haldeman is approximately twice as large. The Lionel lookalike coaching Vosbrinck is named Torin Ferguson. This information I scribble into the book, thanks to the information provided by the excitable public-address announcer. The used-car salesman coaching Haldeman is Holmes McMahan. Before the first pitch, the English teacher from the coffee shop stops by to say hello. Will Sturges. His name's not bad, but he'd make a better Holmes McMahan.

The Vosbrinck catcher laces a double into the right-center field gap on the first pitch that he legs into a triple. He can run. The next three batters strike out. Taiquon Wattson remains on third.

Vosbrinck starts a cocky righthander who thinks he has a fastball but doesn't. The Eagles like to take the first pitch. The pitcher can't throw a strike. The first two batters rap singles. The third tops the ball on a 2-2 count. Wattson hops out from the plate, grabs it barehanded, and throws the guy out at first. One out, runners on second and third. Ryne Standback steps up, fiddling with his batting gloves and showing off his muscles. He takes a strike, right down the middle, and steps out for an eternity before digging back in. The next fastball he yanks 350 feet, fifteen feet foul. High fastball, way out of the zone, Standback lays off. One and two. The Vosbrinck kid throws an outlandish, slow, lollipop curve that Standback could have swung at twice. He whiffs. Either it was pure, dumb luck, or Wattson called a hell of a pitch. The fifth batter then singles and Haldeman gets two runs, anyway.

I find myself paying more attention to Wattson than Standback, who ends up having a decent game. A double and a home run in five at-bats. The home run probably wouldn't have gotten out of a big-league park, but Standback missed it a little, and the bat was aluminum. He dominates high school baseball exactly the way that top prospects always do. The hard thing to measure is how success with that metal bat will translate into a wooden one. Kids don't develop the same feeling of getting good wood on the ball. They just take a rip. If they hit it on the handle, the handle won't break, and the ball might bloop into the outfield. There wasn't anything cheap about Standback's double. I'm not sure he's got the fastest hands in the world, but he's got world-class power. Batting practice showed me that.

Taiquon Wattson doesn't really know how to catch. He hasn't worked on shifting his feet, but his hand-to-eye coordination is extraordinary. Working with a pitcher who can't find the plate, hardly anything gets through. He's got the arm of a shortstop, not to mention the agility. His swing needs a little work, but I wouldn't take it too far away from what's natural. He's relaxed and hits the ball where it's pitched, a virtue I don't see often in kids. He seems smart. What is the deal? Why hasn't he signed a scholarship somewhere? Why doesn't anyone know about him?

Joel Sturmer of the White Sox stops by to tell me the Standback kid's holding a press conference after the game.

"I wasn't aware of any great contingent of the working press," I say.

"I guess it's really a scout conference," Joel says.

"Get a chance to work him out?"

"Oh, no," Joel replies. "Just interview him."

I tell him I appreciate him letting me know. When the game ends -- Haldeman wins, seven to four -- we all stand around and wait for Ryne Standback to get through posing with his teammates and quite a few pretty girls in the same way gangsters might have posed with their tommy guns. The kids all have these mysterious signals they make with their fingers.

Then he proceeds to stroll over and con our asses with all kinds of references to being "blessed" by our presence, and how honored he is to have the Lord Jesus Christ as his copilot. At the same time, he doesn't even hide the fact that it's a con. He's exchanging glances with his worshipful friends, rolling his eyes, and laughing at their sign language, even as he tells us all about his latest victory in Jesus. Half the scouts don't even notice. He's just representing his brand. He won't turn eighteen till April, and he's got a brand.

Because of that waste of time, the Vosbrinck team has already boarded the bus and left by the time I realize that Coach Torin Ferguson promised to tell me a secret about Taiquon Wattson. This is easily rectified because I go home, fill out my report on Ryne Standback, send it to the West Coast via email attachment, and get out of town bright and early so that I'll be otherwise occupied once the Loggers' player-development-and-scouting office reads my observations to the effect that Standback may wind up being a bust on a grand scale if they draft him before the third round.

I get up early Wednesday morning and head straight for Vosbrinck. I've got to get to know Taiquon Wattson and find out why no one else is interested.

CHAPTER 3
Due Diligence

I check in at the front office at Vosbrinck High School, sign the ledger, hang a visitor's lanyard around my neck, identify myself, and ask to see the principal. The receptionist says she is in a meeting, she will see if Mrs. Bauer can spare a few minutes when she returns, and I can have a seat. I notice that I have a text message from the scouting director of the Loggers, Cliff Hueble. I reply -- *Pursuing a lead. Think I found a player. Busy now. Will call asap* -- and start reading a novel, on a German diplomat spying for the Americans during World War II, that I saved on my phone. Not bad. Mrs. Bauer, either. She sweeps into the lobby, nods at me, and walks behind the counter and into her office with the receptionist trailing behind. About ten minutes later, the receptionist says she can see me. I close the novel, pocket the phone, and follow the receptionist.

The principal gets up from her desk and walks around it to greet me. Unnecessarily considerate, I think.

"Hi, I'm Helen Bauer," she says, offering her hand. "I understand you are a scout for the, uh, Portland Loggers. That's a baseball team."

She sits down and asks what she can do for me. I can tell Helen Bauer doesn't have time to spare, so I come straight to the point.

"What can you tell me about Taiquon Wattson?"

"Why, Mr. Kinlaw, Taiquon Wattson is one of my favorite subjects."

"Please call me Clyde," I say. "I never heard of the kid until I watched him play baseball last night in Haldeman. I think he's a pro prospect. I can't believe he hasn't gotten any attention. I hope you can provide me with a reason why."

"Would you like some coffee, Clyde?" she asks.

"Black," I say. "A packet of Sweet 'n' Low."

I sit down and peer at the certificates framed on the wall. Clemson undergraduate. Masters from South Carolina. I can tell I like her better than any principal in any school I attended. Then I think that principals have changed about as much as baseball scouts.

"I understand Taiquon is a three-sport athlete, best on the team in every sport he plays," I say. "What are his plans? Has he signed a scholarship to play football or basketball?"

"Clyde, I'm well aware that this is nothing more than amateur psychology," Helen says, "but it's almost as if Taiquon has a split personality. He tries hard. He just struggles with his academics. He lacks confidence. On the field or court, he is supremely confident."

"I'm no psychologist either, Helen, but he shows quite a bit of intellect, best I can see when he's playing baseball."

"You're exactly right," she says. "His IQ is above average. His grades aren't. He doesn't test well. Our football coach tells me recruiters have shown an interest in him from some junior colleges out in the Midwest -- Oklahoma, Mississippi, Arkansas -- but I think Taiquon feels somewhat humiliated that he can't get in anywhere else. Apparently, he doesn't even want to talk to them."

"Baseball might be an option," I say.

"I hope so," she says. "Taiquon is a sweet kid. He is not dumb. He's just so uncertain of himself, and we've tried several methods, and nothing has worked. I really think he could use some form of therapy, but he's from a very poor family -- most everyone around here is poor -- and there's not much else we can do for him."

Helen invites me to join her for lunch in the cafeteria. It's been a while since I've eaten mystery meat, but the food is prepared reasonably well, and it seems to me the menu hasn't changed in three decades. A breaded patty of undetermined origin. Niblets-style corn. Green beans. A roll. An apple. A half-pint of milk. We sit alone at a table in the back of the room. Teachers are watching, but they're all sitting on the other end of the lunchroom, where undoubtedly Helen Bauer usually sits, too. I'm happy. No one seems to know who I am.

"What worries me," Helen says, "is that I think Taiquon would have a difficult time away from home. He doesn't often articulate his problems. He broods. He freezes up the same way he does in a classroom. If you stick him in some dormitory -- somehow I envision young baseball players lodged in something like a barracks -- and he's probably going to either run away or just withdraw from those around him."

"Most kids today lack self-reliance," I say. "Their parents keep tabs on them that are too close. Don't let them ride their bikes around town. Just let 'em play video games all day long. Lots of the kids I see remind me of robots or something. Very few of them are dumb. They've just got out of the habit of thinking."

"That may be a bit of a jaded view," Helen says, "but I can see why you feel that way. Taiquon doesn't have a cell, doesn't have a video console, doesn't have a driver's license, rides the bus to school."

"How's he get home from practice?" I ask.

"He catches a ride most days. Either that, or he walks. He lives in some run-down apartments on the other side of town. It's just two or three miles."

"I understand your concerns," I say. "I paid pretty close attention to him yesterday in Haldeman. He's got extraordinary athletic ability. It is tough to go off and play ball away from home. The minor leagues aren't as tough as they used to be, but they're still tough for kids who've never been away from home. On the other hand, I think it's fair to say that baseball has a lot of experience with taking kids from far-flung backgrounds and bringing them along. Every team has kids from Latin America. Most of them can't speak a word of English when they get here, and we put 'em in places like Kingsport, Tennessee, and Batavia, New York. I spent a summer in Billings, Montana. I'm gonna talk to him, Helen, and see what I think."

"Did you come down here on your own, Clyde?"

"I did."

"I sincerely hope you can do something for Taiquon," she says.

So, I've got this ballplayer savant on my hands.

"I'd have bet I wouldn't have seen you no more," Torin Ferguson says. He's untangling a water hose as I stroll down to the Vosbrinck diamond."

"He's a prospect, maybe," I say. "I liked what I saw."

"Why come you didn't look me up after the game?"

"My assignment was the Standback kid. By the time I got through with that hullabaloo, you and your team had already left."

"Hullabaloo" is a word of which Torin Ferguson lacks knowledge. What's wonderful is it doesn't matter. "Hullabaloo" couldn't mean anything other than what it is.

"You talked to Helen Bauer about him," Ferguson says.

"Standard procedure," I reply. "Word gets around."

"It's always a good idea to maintain a working relationship with your principal."

"Yeah, I can see that," I say. "I believe you were going to tell me why Taiquon Wattson plays catcher."

Ferguson smiles. "It's right there in that bag." He points into the dugout. We walk over. He empties the cloth sack. It has catcher's gear in it, along with a couple of bats and a handful of balls.

"See that mitt," Ferguson says. "Taiquon doesn't own a glove. We provide a catcher's mitt. That's why he's been catching for four years."

"I'll be damned," I say. "I must've gone back in time. Kid plays catcher because he can't afford a glove. Doesn't own a cell phone. Next thing you're gonna tell me is that he doesn't have a PlayStation."

"I'm satisfied he doesn't," Ferguson says.

I have to sit down. This isn't a scouting assignment. It's *The Twilight Zone*.

I tell Ferguson I'll be back in touch and walk back to the truck. I discover, a bit to my surprise, that my binoculars are behind the seat, resting in front of the benches Ford claims people can sit in. I don't remember putting them there. It's one of those automatic habits that are only noticeable when some glitch occurs and they don't get done. I inexplicably take the binoculars in the house, and then I don't put them back in the truck the next morning. This time I did.

Vosbrinck is flat, near the Georgia border and Strom Thurmond Lake, which, I believe, they still call Clarks Hill on the other side of it because Thurmond was a South Carolina politician and in spite of the fact that another reservoir is named after Georgia's Richard B. Russell, and it's behind the next dam up the Savannah River. The high school is surrounded by forests on all sides, except for a strip of grass around the entry road, and what is carved out of the woods is barren and more dirt than grass. I drive down the left-field line and park on a small asphalt road between the football stadium and the baseball field. While the team members are drifting out to the diamond, starting to stretch, I take out my cell and ring Frank Staley, Jr., the assistant player development director of the Portland Loggers. It's lunchtime on the West Coast, and, if I know Frank Junior, he's eating at his desk from a paper bag he brought from home. Frank Senior and I were close. I spent some time fishing with Frank Junior when he was just a kid. Now he's the only man in the front office who pays any attention to me, and he probably has to hide it.

He sees my name on his phone and answers.

"What kind of sandwich today, kid?" I ask him.

"Smoked turkey and provolone on wheat," he says, laughing. "You know me too well, Clyde."

"Yeah, well, I pay attention to intangibles," I say. "How'd my report go over?"

"It's not every day I read a report on a prospect that suggests that he is 'intellectually dishonest'," Frank Junior says. "You been taking psychology classes on the side?"

"I read a little," I say. "The Standback kid's a bullshitter. Everybody around him – his old man, his coach – is one, too. I looked at the coach, Holmes something or other, and I thought his eyes were green. Turns out they're dollar marks. I filled in all the numbers. Kid's got the tools to be great, all right, but, when he's feeding you a line, he doesn't even try to hide it. He's exactly the type you waste a bunch of money on, and he burns out in Double-A. But that's not why I called."

"Your side project," Frank Junior says.

"I want you to check your database and whatever other databases you have access to, and see if there's anything there on a kid named Taiquon – that's T-A-I-Q-U-O-N – Wattson – two T's, W-A-T-T-S-O-N – in Vosbrinck, South Carolina. He's gonna need a lot of work, but he might be something special. I'm about to watch him practice now."

"You're hiding in a bunch of trees with a pair of binoculars," Frank Junior says.

"You know me too well, too, kid," I say. "No, seriously, I'm sitting in my truck out beyond the outfield fence. Yeah. I got my binoculars."

"Don't ever change, Clyde," Frank Junior says. "Keep me posted."

This shy, withdrawn kid, this loner, is bouncing around like Stephon Curry in a gym. He's joking around, chattering, while he catches batting practice. When he takes his turn at the plate, he ropes one line drive after another. Then he gets under one. The park is deep down the lines, but the fence isn't curved, and it's shallow in the power alleys. The ball bounces in front of the truck and bounces over it. It would be a cheap home run if I wasn't sitting 100 feet behind the fence.

I find myself getting excited. Just filling in reports on can't-miss prospects is getting old. I need to pull off a coup. I need to take a kid under my wing and develop him myself. I used to play big-league ball. I like the privacy but miss the respect. I used to be somebody. What is there about Taiquon Wattson that renders him unnoticed? I don't know that he isn't on drugs, or that he doesn't have two kids running around, or that doesn't knock off liquor stores in his spare time, but I can't see any signs of it, at least not through binoculars.

When it looks as if the practice is winding down, I put the binoculars away, get out of the truck, and walk around the ballpark's fence. I'm stiff as a board from sitting still for two hours, so I walk slowly, trying to get my knees limber. I walk through the gate near the end of the visitor's dugout and make sure Ferguson sees me. He talks to his team for a couple of minutes and apparently tells Taiquon Wattson that I need to talk to him. The kid trots over as his teammates head off in the other direction.

"Sit down, Taiquon," I say. "Do you know anything about me?"

Now the happy-go-lucky ballplayer looks as his coach just told him to report to the principal's office. It seems difficult for him to blurt out two words: "Naw, suh."

"My name is Clyde Kinlaw. I work on the side as a scout for the Portland Loggers. Many years ago, I played first base for them. Spent six years in Portland. Later on, I coached and managed in the minors, and I spent five years managing the big club. Five years ago, they fired me. I reckon I'm sort of semi-retired, even though I don't want to be. Now I live up in Youngville. It's my hometown. I live by myself. Ain't got much family around anymore. I just go out and do a little scouting."

I wait for Taiquon to say something. He's trying to think of something.

"Are you in the Hall of Fame?" he asks finally.

I laugh. "Not even close, son. I did all right, though."

He hasn't looked at me enough to describe anything above my sneakers. When Helen Bauer said it was like he had a split personality, she wasn't joking.

"I watched you play up in Haldeman last night," I say. "I like what I saw. I'm gonna watch you play some more. Have you ever thought about playing ball for a career?"

"Not baseball," he says.

"You got any plans to play anything else once you graduate?"

"Naw, suh."

"Well, I just wanted to meet you," I say. "I don't want to hold you up. I just wanted to know I was looking at you, and we'll just see what happens. You got a ride home, Taiquon?"

"I can walk."

"No, it's no problem. Just run along, and when you get out of the shower, I'll be waiting for you outside."

When Taiquon gets in, I ask him if he's hungry. He says, yeah, but his grandmother has him something fixed. I ask if there's a place in town where a man can buy an ice cream cone. He says there's a place on Highway 7, and I buy him a cone of vanilla. My taste is a bit more specialized, and I order butter pecan.

He gives me directions, and I ask him if he lives with his grandmother. He says, yeah. When I ask him if he has any brothers and sisters, he says six, but they're all older than him, and they've been in Atlanta since his mother moved there. He doesn't volunteer much, but at least I've got him talking in sentences. He lives in an old frame house in what looks like it used to be a mill neighborhood. At least it's not an apartment in the projects. Not much good comes from those places. He says thanks and gets out, doesn't invite me in, and I tell him, next time I'm down here, I'll take him and his granny out to eat, wherever they like. His expression leads me to believe he doesn't know whether he wants to take me up on that or not.

CHAPTER 4
A Reason for Nothing

Frank Staley Jr. calls and says there isn't a trace of information regarding a Taiquon Wattson of Vosbrinck, South Carolina.

"It doesn't seem possible," he says.

"He's a lot more known as a football player, best I can tell," I say. "Vosbrinck's the kind of town where there's not much attention on anything but football, if that. It's a poor county. Taiquon's a quarterback, but his grades aren't good enough to get into a decent college. He's painfully shy. The principal says his I.Q. is above average, but he struggles in school and his test scores are a disaster. She says he's not dumb, but it's almost like he's got a split personality. On the field, he's got all the confidence in the world, but he's insecure or something about mental things. I could've told her that from watching him play baseball. I watched him practice, and then I talked to him, bought him an ice cream cone, and gave him a ride home. It's true. It's like a light switches off when he walks off the field."

"And he's got the tools?"

"He's got the tools, Junior, but he's not ready for pro ball," I say. "I'm not even sure he's willing to try. His mother took her other six kids and moved to Atlanta. She left Taiquon behind to take care of his grandmother. He's a really gifted athlete, but he plays catcher, and he doesn't know how to catch because nobody's ever taught him how."

"So ... what does that mean? He's not ready for pro ball. What do you propose?"

"Well, I haven't made up my mind just yet," I say. "I've got to get to know the kid better, but I sort of want to take him under my wing and see if I can get him ready … make a player out of him."

"So … I take it you want to take a leave of absence from scouting," Frank Junior says.

"I don't draw a salary from the club. I don't reckon I've got a leave to take."

Frank Junior pauses for, oh, ten seconds. "You are correct, Clyde."

"Come to think of it," I say, "I don't think there's anything to keep me from polishing this diamond in the rough and placing his services on the open market if I can get Taiquon to trust me enough to do that."

"You wouldn't do that, Clyde. You wouldn't do that to me."

"You're right, Junior. I'm a fool, but you're right. I don't trust anybody in Portland other than you, but I don't trust anybody at all anywhere else. I don't want you to talk it up. Ain't nobody else in the front office who does anything but laugh when my name comes up, anyhow. Don't tell nobody, and the whole notion – me taking some obscure black kid and making a prospect out of him – won't get ridiculed."

"You are so wrong about that," Frank Junior says.

"You don't lie worth a shit, Junior. I appreciate the effort, though."

"Stay in touch, Clyde. If you get this kid to a point where I need to see him, let me know. I'll figure out a way to get down there, and you and I can work him out."

"I hope it comes to that, Junior. I appreciate you. Bye, now."

The stakes have just gotten higher. I'm taking a big chance here. If I put all my effort into turning Taiquon Wattson into a prospect, and I'm wrong, and he isn't one, or he doesn't have the desire, it'll hurt me, if not in the eyes of the Portland Loggers in general – they all think I'm a fool who can't adapt to change – then in the eyes of Frank Staley, Jr., the last ally I've got in Portland and quite possibly anywhere else. I used to hit him grounders and play pepper with him when he was twelve or, thirteen years old. Now he's a whiz kid of player development, and he's working his way up the ladder with the team his old man owned and brought to Portland when he was five years old.

Junior still thinks a lot of me. He's got enough sense not to spread it around, but he knows that I can tell a prospect when I see one. He can read charts and graphs, too.

I decide to give Taiquon a rest for a day. I'm feeling some pressure. I love this kid. He's poor, and he's got his grandmama to tend to, and I expect a heap of folks around Vosbrinck have him pegged as just another kid who's going to be hanging out on a street corner one day with nothing left except what might have been. I know what they're saying. *That boy is some kind of athlete. What a shame he's dumb as a mudhole.* I grew up with kids like Taiquon, but what sets him apart is he seems to be so innocent. He's a mystery, one who seems too good to be true. I don't know enough about him. For all I know, he keeps his grandmama's bills paid by selling weed on the side. I don't believe it. It's not the way I read him, but, if I decide to make this leap of faith, I've got to know I'm right. It may be my last shot to regain some respect in baseball. If I go into this wide-open and fail, I'll have plenty of time to hang out at Vern Crosley's Office Supply and talk about the good, old days, and that's all that mine will be.

Naturally, that's exactly what I do. I tell Vern for the umpteenth time about the time I hit for the cycle at Olympic Stadium back before the Expos left Montreal and the time I doubled in the tying run at the All-Star Game in Anaheim. Henry Locklear raises hell about why the City of Youngville won't move the historical marker so he can turn right onto South Broad Street from Jacobs Highway. Henry had a fender bender there about a year ago, and he's been complaining about it ever since. I reckon I sympathize with him. One day I'm going to be too old to drive, too. Danny Kinard, who used to promote the dirt track, gives me his latest take on how NASCAR got so screwed up. At about three in the afternoon, I walk around the corner to the coffee shop and bakery and sit by myself, sipping on some Breakfast Blend and nibbling on two cinnamon walnut muffins. Some folks like Danishes. Some like bagels. Some like cupcakes. I'm a muffin man, natural born. The coffee shop closes at four, and there's nobody I know there. I read a couple of chapters of a book on my cell, and then I decide to drive down to Johncock's Pharmacy because I need some tincture of iodine and the collection of assorted Band-Aids that always seems to run out just about right. I also buy a multivitamin so that my urine stays expensive and fortified, and Wells Johncock and I whisper to each other about how screwed up the country is. Both of us don't much care for the current president, but most folks around here like him, so we hold it down because political agitation is bad for business, and it's hard enough already for an independent druggist to stave off the chain stores trying to close him down. Twice a week, I get a recording on my machine about how much cheaper it will be if I go to CVS to get my medications refilled, and I wouldn't sell out Wells if his pharmacy cost me double. The conversation alone is worth a lot.

It occurs to me that I haven't had any Mexican in a while, so I hit happy hour at Poza Rica, where I order a jumbo margarita and tell Humberto to fix me up whatever he's in the mood to cook. He never disappoints, at least not until nature calls loudly the next morning. As luck would have it, Vera Hill is at the bar. She was a Hill in high school. Like me, she's been divorced twice since. I don't even know whom she married. I was off playing ball. Now neither one of us is interested in further romantic entanglements, and that's what makes her a good female partner in a Mexican joint. I've got a right good buzz when I get through with the massive margarita and Humberto's steaming carnitas that he fixed because he had "had some real fresh pork." Vera and I have been talking about how worried she is about her good-looking daughter, who's running around with an ex-basketball star who dropped out of Limestone a semester shy of graduation. Vera says she doesn't have a bit of a problem with Regina dating a black boy, but she's got a suspicion the two of them are up to no good, and nowadays folks don't mind interracial relationships unless the two relating interracially ain't no count.

"I, on the other hand, have a daughter who married a podiatrist, and all I get from her is a Facebook happy birthday once a year," I say. "At least Regina talks to you, even if she doesn't make no sense."

"Kids," Vera says. "You can't do a thing with them."

"That's a fact," I reply. "Try to give them advice, and they absolutely will do the opposite. I've learned not to preach to mine. If Marian or Cam asks me what I think, they might listen to what I've got to say, but there comes a point where you just got to let them learn their own lessons, I reckon. It's all I can figure."

I tell Vera I've got to go, so I give her a hug and a peck on the cheek. I should have paid more attention to her when we were young, but when I got drafted and shipped off to instructional league, I left way too much behind me, most likely because I was just as hardheaded then as my own estranged children are now.

I don't feel seriously impaired, but I'm careful on the way home to take a path through the streets and not the highways. I've never been caught drunk driving, even when I was a young ballplayer and deserved to be, and this would be an inauspicious time in my life to start. I fix myself a coffee when I get home and sit down to watch the Loggers play Milwaukee in a spring training replay from the afternoon being replayed on MLB TV. Javon McRae pitches four innings and still looks to me like he's out of shape, but he doesn't give up but a run, and the Loggers wind up winning, 6-4, and that completes the nothing day I'm having because my mind is subconsciously occupied ruminating about Taiquon Wattson.

CHAPTER 5

A Man I Trust

*I*t's Thursday. Taiquon Wattson has a game tomorrow night against Priestlyville. I don't have much desire to watch him practice. I might wander over to Jernigan College this afternoon. No particular reason except just to think. The problem with going to a game here in town is that people who know me – and everyone knows me here – will think I have a reason. I know better than to sit in the stands, even though it's the only place where I can see the whole field. The Green Hornets play in a park built to play in, not watch. Since the dugouts aren't "dug out," they block the views of fans sitting behind them. If I go early, I can stake out a spot for my folding chair on a mound between the stands and the third-base non-dugout, but sometimes there's a pop-up tent erected in that space for the purpose of a radio broadcast. Such a tent is always present on the first-base side, which is why the only possible alternative to the stands behind the plate is the mound behind the third-base line. Even then, I can't see down the left-field line. Once in a while, scouts show up at Jernigan. They sit behind the plate, of course. By sitting alone, or in the company of an old friend, I lessen the perception that I'm there for any productive reason.

It could be that I think about such matters way too much, particularly since I don't see any scouts in the grandstand.

Scouts are swarming all over the high schools now, filing their detailed reports and awaiting evaluations from their clubs. The minor leagues will start playing in a week or two. The scouts who draw a salary from big-league organizations will spend more of their time watching their own players and those of other clubs who might be involved in trades when a sagging big-league club sells out its present and dumps salaries in exchange for prospects. That way, the struggling organization can sell off those players in a few years when they start making decent money. This ebbs and flows. The fans turn on a cheapskate owner. He either spends money or sells out. Most organizations are like mine. The Loggers' goal is to win economically. They try to put a good team together and make the most of it quickly before the star players take their services to New York or Los Angeles or Chicago. It got bad in Portland when I was playing. That's why the Loggers shipped me to Toronto, and that's where my knees started going bad on the artificial turf. That fall I walked off the field in October in the prime of my career, and by the All-Star Break of the following year, I was washed up.

I'm not bitter. It's the way it works. *Them's the breaks.*

I drag my chair out of its canvas bag. I set it up tilted a little downhill, the better to get up and down. A couple of years ago, I went to the doctor, figuring he'd just tell me I needed a little arthroscopic surgery to clean it out. What he said was that all he could do to my knee was replace it, and he might as well replace both of them because the other one, the left, wasn't much better. My knees have been cut on enough. I'm not going to do it till I have to.

Two elderly people, a man and a woman, are sitting to my left, both in wheelchairs. The game is in the third inning. Jernigan is playing North Carolina A&T. It's 4-4 and the Hornets have two men on and one out. JC is wearing uniforms modeled after the Los Angeles Dodgers, only green where the Dodgers are blue and gold where the Dodgers are red. Like the Dodgers, the white on their shirts and pants are bright and clean. I like that, not so much the Dodgers – or the Green Hornets – but the uniforms. I overhear the man and woman talking to each other. They make little sense. They could be mentally handicapped. They could be stroke victims. They could have Alzheimer's. It's wonderful that they're at the game, but I don't see much hope for conversation. When I walked in, I didn't pay much attention to my surroundings, other than craning my neck to see if there were any scouts behind the plate. I was lost in thought. Now I see Virgil Scurry sitting in his folding chair about ten yards farther up the third-base line. He's exactly whom I need to see. I catch his eyes. He waves. I pick up my chair and its bag and walk down to where he's sitting, watching as a kid from JC hits a home run to make it 7-4. There may be forty fans scattered about. When the modest applause subsides, I sit my chair down next to Virgil.

"Mind the company?" I ask.

"Not at all," he replies.

Jernigan College is a small school of less than a thousand students, yet its athletic teams reside near the bottom of NCAA Division I in a conference known inexplicably as the Big South. Virgil Scurry is a retired black businessman, active in the community, who likes baseball and, based on past conversations, golf. The extent of our knowledge of each other is defined by the conversations we've had over the past few years at Green Hornets baseball games. On those occasions when I watch a baseball game without notes to take and observations to remember, I find it the best place on earth at that moment to engage in conversation. Alone among the team sports, watching baseball is relaxing.

Our paths don't cross more than two or three times each spring. Almost every time, Virgil looks at my purple-and-yellow LSU chair and says, "I didn't know you were an LSU fan."

Every time I reply, "I'm not. Remember? I bought this chair when I was driving across Louisiana, and I needed a folding chair, and the one with LSU on it cost ten dollars less than the camouflage one. I don't have anything against LSU, but I've got this chair because I'm cheap."

And Virgil replies, "That's right. Now I remember."

The inning ends. I think Virgil is talking to himself until I notice he's wearing earbuds.

"End of the fourth," he says. "Jernigan eight, A&T four."

Is he reporting inning-by-inning scores to some website? Of course not.

"My nephew went to A&T," he says. "I just try to keep him posted."

As North Carolina A&T is a predominantly black school – if I'm not mistaken, the term HBCU stands for Historically Black Colleges and Universities – it reminds me of a phenomenon I noticed at another game here.

"I saw something a few years ago that I've never seen before," I say.

"Oh, yeah?"

"I believe JC was playing North Carolina Central," I say. "JC had all white players and a black head coach. Central had all black players and a white head coach."

"Is that right? I remember that game, but I didn't notice."

"Why you must be color-blind," I say, smiling.

We talk about politics for a while. He knows I'm not particularly political, but what little politics I've got is Democratic in a place where most whites don't admit to being anything other than Republican. Virgil gives me the lowdown on several candidates for local political office. All I know is most of the names, and those come from emails I somehow absorb at the same time I'm deleting them.

The Aggies get back in the game. It's 8-6 after five.

"What have you been doing?" Virgil asks. "Found any prospects out there?"

"Well, Virgil, I'm kind of glad I bumped into you. I didn't come out here looking for you, but I'm glad you just happened to be here," I say. "Most of what I do is just evaluate a prospect the big club assigns me, but I was watching a kid from Haldeman the other day, and I noticed a black kid from Vosbrinck that nobody seems to know about. He's got me kind of fascinated."

"Oh, yeah?" Virgil says that a lot.

I tell him about how the kid's more known for his football and basketball ability, and how he's poor and hasn't got much opportunity because he hasn't the grades to get a scholarship anywhere other than junior colleges out in the Midwest, and I think he's got the tools to play pro baseball, but he's raw, and I'm right fascinated by him, and I'm thinking about taking him under my wing and trying to make a big leaguer out of him.

"What do you get out of it?" Virgil inquires.

"Oh, the usual," I say. "Bonus from the big club. Mainly, though, I want to prove I can do it. I've found this kid nobody knows about, and I don't want anybody to know about him, because I don't want to see him short-changed, signed for nothing, and wasted filling out minor-league rosters till they lose interest in him because they ain't got much money invested."

Virgil takes all this in. We watch a half-inning in silence. After the Green Hornets go down in order in the sixth, I tell him about how Taiquon lives with his grandmother, and his siblings are in Atlanta with his mother, and how he plays catcher because the team supplies a mitt, and how he's so full of joy on the field and so withdrawn off it.

"What are you planning to do?" Virgil asks.

"Well, I don't know," I say. "If I'm gonna go full in on this kid, I gotta believe it can be done. I'm thinking. That's what I came out here for. To think. I'll tell you what one of my concerns is, and this is something I can't really talk to anybody about, at least not many folks."

"What's that?"

"I've seen this happen before," I say. "There's a racial barrier. I'm white. He's black. I've gotta get him to trust me. Race becomes an issue. Several times I've stuck my neck out on a black kid, scouted him, pushed him to the front office, and then had some other scout, a black man, swoop in and charm his family, sign the kid for ten cents on the dollar of what he is worth, and then ship him off to instructional league, where the kid's likely to get in over his head, and, pretty soon, he's back home, and if he's lucky, learning how to work in heating and air conditioning or something. Taking on this kid, and doing it right, is going to take lots of trust between us."

"Well," Virgil says, "I expect only you can make that call."

"Yep. That's what I think, too. I don't suppose if this moves along, and I decide to take this kid on and work with him, you'd like to meet him?"

"I don't make it down to Vosbrinck much," he says. "I can't remember the last time, you want to know the truth."

"Ain't no need to get ahead of ourselves," I say. "I don't suppose you got a business card on you."

Virgil reaches into the zip-up compartment in his blue PC windbreaker. He hands me a simple card, black letters on white, and it's the first time I know what he does now that he's supposed to be retired. The card is for a mortuary.

"It's my nephew's," Virgil says. "I helped set him up in business. I guess you'd say I'm a consultant."

That's what the card says, too. I hand Virgil mine, with its Portland Loggers logo that identifies me as "a scouting consultant," which, translated, means "he ain't on the payroll."

Then we go back to talking about what a lunatic our president is, how the Republicans are hard to beat because they've got so much money, and how if the Democrats are going to win a statewide office, this is the year, but we both agree that it still isn't likely.

I tell Virgil I'm tired of Democrats who think they can win elections by being just a wee bit less conservative than the Republicans. I tell him if we're going to lose, we might as well go down fighting. Virgil is a careful man. He just nods.

The Green Hornets win the game, twelve to eight, and I drive out to the Pilot Truck Center for twenty dollars worth of gas, which ought to be enough to get me to Vosbrinck and back tomorrow, and I use a coupon to buy a foot-long cheesy chicken and bacon at the Subway inside. I got some Pringles and Diet Pepsi at the house, where I watch the Loggers play the Arizona Diamondbacks on the MLB Channel and read *The Youngville Chronicle* and the *Brouillette County Advertiser* while I'm munching on my sub.

CHAPTER 6

The Right Stuff

It's Torin Ferguson who tells me my talk with Taiquon Wattson has had a profound effect on him, but I can't tell. As I watch him warm up for a Friday night game against Abbeville, he seems relaxed and enthusiastic.

"If Taiquon had a glove, would you pitch him?" I ask.

"If a game was on the line, I would," Torin says. "I don't know who would catch. I don't know if I've got anybody who *could* catch him. You've seen him throw to second. He can throw the ball a good bit harder than anybody else on the team."

While we're chatting next to the dugout, Taiquon is in the outfield, inexplicably, shagging flies with his catcher's mitt. A white, freckle-faced kid hammers a batting-practice fastball deep into the left-center field gap, farther than it looks like he can hit it. Taiquon tracks it down, perhaps twenty feet from the fence where its direction turns across the center. It's likely the deepest part of the park, maybe 370 feet from the plate. He catches it backhanded and slides across the grass shy of the warning track. He holds on, too. With a mitt.

"You know what they call his hands?" I say.

"What?"

"Soft. A boy either got those or he doesn't."

"You really think he's got a chance?" Torin asks.

"Taiquon needs work," I reply. "If he went straight to Instructional League, base level of pro ball, it'd eat him alive.

He'd fall through the cracks. They'd say, yeah, he's got ability, but that's what everybody down here has."

"You still here," Torin said. "What's your plan?"

"I'm thinking," I say. "I haven't brought up Taiquon but with one person in the organization, the one fellow the Loggers got who still listens to me. I'm taking a leave of absence, they'd say, but I'm not a salaried scout. Truth is, I can do whatever I want. I'm not broke. I'm not rich as an ex-big-leaguer ought to be, either, but I make enough to get me by. I need a challenge. Taiquon's a challenge. If I just needed a few bucks, I'd make some big push to get Taiquon's name on a contract once your season's over, and it wouldn't be much money, and the likelihood is that all he'd do is fill out a roster, and the club wouldn't give him the attention he needs because they ain't got much money in him."

"And you ain't got no competition?"

"If I do, I'd say you know it."

"I ain't heard a word from nobody," Torin says.

"I'm glad. I'm kind of amazed at it myself. My problem is figuring out a way to get him the instruction he needs, and, at the same time, not tip off other scouts who don't have a clue about his potential. I haven't got an answer of how to do that yet, but I'm thinking about it an awful lot."

"I appreciate anything you can do for Taiquon, Clyde. He's the best athlete I got. I let him do what he wants to do. I know I don't know enough to give him the instruction he needs. I love baseball, but I'm a football coach. I come here because I'm in line to be the head football coach when Coach Tarkenton retires after one more year. When you coach high school, you wear a lot of hats. I coach J.V. basketball, too."

"I'd say you wear–em right well," I say.

It's a sloppy game that Vosbrinck wins, 8-6. I don't keep score, but I just tally up errors and count fourteen between the two teams. Taiquon lets a couple of wild pitches slip through, but all three of the pitchers Torin sends out to the mound are all over the place. Taiquon gets two hits and drives in one, but he does seem a little distracted. Twice he takes a called strike three, both times with no one on base and two out. He walks once, steals two bases, and scores three runs. He's average by his standards but by far the best player on the field.

When it's over, Taiquon and his teammates – and the three coaches – are involved in pulling up the bases and sweeping the mound. I walk through the gate and wait beyond the dugout. Taiquon is looking at the ground when he finally walks over, looking as if he dreads it.

"I wasn't too good," he says.

"You're fine," I say. "You did your best. The team won the game. That's the main thing. What are you doing tomorrow?"

"I gotta put up groceries at the Food Lion in the morning."

"When you go to work?"

"Eight o'clock."

"And when you knock off?" He doesn't volunteer much.

"'Round about two," he says.

"You reckon you can ride over to Bluefield and back with me?" I ask.

"Yes, sir."

"I'll pick you up in the parking lot at two." I don't volunteer much, either.

On the way back to Youngville, it's about nine-thirty when I reach Bluefield. I stop for supper at the O'Charley's and look up the local sporting goods options. When I'm through eating a fried-chicken salad, I drive through the parking lot of a Hibbetts so that I don't have to worry about how to get there tomorrow afternoon.

It occurs to me that it might be taboo for me to buy a kid some equipment. I've never heard of a pro scout getting in trouble about something like that, though. It's not like I'm a Clemson alumnus buying him a Mustang under the table. A long time ago, when I was playing in the big leagues, I shared a golf cart with a college basketball coach, and, after quite a few beers, we became friends. He told me there were degrees of cheating.

"Oh, yeah?" I said.

"Years ago, I was an assistant with an old veteran coach," he said. "No need to say his name."

"I don't have no need to know."

"One time, he called me into his office, and he had a bunch of expensive clothes," the basketball coach – his name was Todd Marable, as I recall – said. When I got in there, he was going through each box, removing the clothes – there were sport coats, dress shirts, pants, polo shirts – and wadding them up.

"Ah, he told me, take these old things out in the locker room, and see if the boys want any of 'em. The point he made was that there's a difference between giving clothes to a poor kid who ain't got nothing to wear and buying a kid by puttin' him in a set of wheels. They're both cheating, technically, but one is really just showing some human compassion."

A baseball player who hasn't got a fielding glove is in the category of human compassion, I think. Besides, I've got to spend some time with Taiquon and try to get him out of his shell. I can't get him to trust me by buying him some gear, but it might break some ice.

CHAPTER 7

A Modest Investment

Vosbrinck is starting to feel like my daily commute. It's a little over an hour away. Until last week, I could probably count on one hand the times I've been there. When I was in high school, I think it was Strom Thurmond Lake where a friend and I went fishing. Back then, it was just as likely to be called Clarks Hill. Once Thurmond died, folks stopped quibbling about it. I think there's a golf course somewhere around there. I never played any team sport down there, though I passed through Augusta, Ga., which isn't far away, a few times in the minor leagues.

When a man becomes a professional athlete, his river overruns its banks. The old Savannah is an extreme example. Dams stop it up most of the way down the border of South Carolina and Georgia, but then the gates open, and it runs free. When I went fishing on Thurmond Lake, I was in the minors, and it was fall, and I'd just gotten done playing a whole season in upper-Class A. There's an upper and a lower A. The next year I was in Double-A, and then I skipped a class and wound up in the bigs, the show, and all of a sudden, I was making money, big money, and I outgrew fishing trips with my hometown buddies. I started going deep-sea fishing off the coast of Puerto Rico and hunting in the wintry Rockies. I moved to Florida in the offseason, even though I was playing on the diametrically opposite side of the country.

I chased women and married two of them with disastrous consequences. My kids barely know me. I'm still bitter about being fired as manager of the Loggers. I had a winning record, overall, but things got worse the final year after the club sold the best players out from under me. The front-office pencil pushers I thought were my friends whispered that I had a drinking problem. It was a way to pave the road to my firing, a way to justify it. I didn't have a drinking problem. I drank. I didn't get drunk. A couple of beers on the road helped me sleep. I didn't even know any of the players were there that night in Arlington when two of them got in a fight. The story hit the papers, and when my name was on a police report, it was just another stigma attached to my file.

I don't know why I'm fixated on that incident now. One of the players in the fight was from Venezuela. I sympathize with the Latino kids. They find themselves all alone in a vast country that speaks a language they don't understand when they get here. One reason they get a reputation for being difficult, erratic, and sulky is that they learn a simplistic version of English. They don't understand the nuances. Every word has one meaning, and, sometimes, when someone else uses one of those words, the kid only knows the harsh one. Some grow angry out of frustration. Others just confide in the other Spanish-speaking players who are in the same fix. I think about it because I realize that Taiquon Wattson might be another breed of the same cat. He doesn't have a driver's license, let alone a car. He has a bicycle. He doesn't have a cell or a PlayStation. He's never played Fortnite, whatever that is. My kid wanted Fortnite for his birthday. Naturally, I bought the wrong version or something. I gave him two hundred bucks and told him to buy what he wanted. I'm out of touch with my son. Taiquon is out of touch with almost everything around him. I can't get back in touch with Terry. Maybe I can get through to Taiquon. He likes baseball. I'm not sure I want to know what Terry likes.

I park in an open area of the lot so that I have an unobstructed view of the Food Lion's automatic doors. I'm fifteen minutes early, and Taiquon apparently gets off ten minutes late. Till two o'clock, I open the window and cut the engine off so that I can read email on my cell. It takes most of the time just deleting the junk I don't want to read. I start thinking Taiquon is a no-show. I don't doubt he's scared, but I don't size him up as a liar. Sure enough, he shows up outside the entrance, staring around. I crank up the engine and drive over. I stop right in front of him, but he's got his hand over his eyes, squinting and looking into the distance. I push the button and lower the passenger-side window.

"Hey! Taiquon!"

He sees me and feels stupid.

"Hop in," I say.

I've got to be careful with this kid. I don't overwhelm him with personality, but I don't want to get into a silent standoff, either. He isn't going to trust me just because I've got a smiling face. I don't blame him. My smiling face is white. If I were in his shoes, I wouldn't trust me, either. A man's got to earn respect; he doesn't just get it.

"You eaten?" I ask.

"No, sir. I'm ah'ight'ough."

I'm all right, though.

"Good." I smile. "I reckon there's a heap more places to choose from in Bluefield. I just thought we'd take a ride over there and back and try to get to know each other. I don't know whether you got what it takes to play big-league ball. You don't know if I got enough sense to tell. What's your favorite kind of food, Taiquon?"

"I love catfish," he says.

"Me, too. If you got a favorite place to eat, it suits me."

"Don't matter. I don't get over that way much."

We don't talk for a few minutes while I'm getting out of town.

I break the silence by saying, "Taiquon, do you love baseball enough to play it every night?"

"I love any sport that much," he says.

"That's good 'cause it ain't easy. Sometimes you play a doubleheader, then have to get on the bus and ride through the night to the next town. It's hard to get your rest."

"Yes, sir." That's it. I try to think of something else to say. I pull off at a Little Cricket.

"How 'bout something to drink? What do you like?"

"Mountain Dew," he says. I go in and come back with a Dew for him and a Diet Dr. Pepper for myself.

Once we get back on the road, I say, "Taiquon, I don't expect you to trust me because you don't know enough yet. If I can get you a shot at playing pro ball, I'll get a bonus for doing it, but I swear, I ain't gonna get rich off it, and the reason I'm taking this interest in you isn't 'cause of money, it's 'cause I've seen enough ability in you that I believe you might have a shot. I don't want you to trust me till I prove I'm worthy of your trust. You know what I'm saying?"

"Yes, sir." Polite kid. Always says, sir and ma'am. I just wish he'd say something else now and then.

"Now, that works in return, too. I'm gonna be honest with you. You ask me a question, and I'm gonna tell you what I think. Once I convince you this is true, I'm gonna want you to trust me and be honest in return," I say.

"Yes, sir." Taiquon almost stammers. "I trust you, Mr. Kinlaw."

I'll get him to start calling me Clyde down the road. I'm not going to try to impress him with my big-league credentials. Every now and then, I may use something that happened to me to make a point, but we're going to have to get closer before that will do any good.

"I know you live with your grandmother," I say. "Can she get by without you around?"

"She probably does better without me," Taiquon replies. "I'm satisfied I cost her more money than she gets from me. Ma, she ain't old or nothing. She ain't nothin' but fifty-five."

We go to O'Charley's, mainly because I like that chain, and I know they've got decent catfish. It turns out I'm wrong, and, for whatever reason, it's not on the menu anymore. I hold up the menu to the waitress and point at the whitefish fillets, and, if Taiquon knows any different, he's not saying. I'm pretty sure the seasoned, light breading will satisfy him. I order the same fried chicken salad I had two nights ago. I could use a beer, but I'm on my best behavior, so I get Diet Dr. Pepper. That's another thing I like about O'Charley's. They serve it. I also order some fried pepper jack cheese wedges to split with Taiquon. He stares at them as if they were escargots, but I show him how to dip them in the marinara sauce, and the look on his face suggests that he finds it quite the taste sensation. He's quite hungry. I had a pack of Lance crackers and a pint of chocolate milk coming down the road from Youngville, but it didn't leave much of a dent in my appetite, either. We don't talk a lot.

When we get back to the truck, Taiquon volunteers something for the first time.

"I ain't never et no fish without bones in 'em," he says.

I think a minute and realize that growing up off Thurmond Lake, a good portion of the fish he's eaten have been the fish he's caught. I get over my initial shock.

"It's called a fillet," I say. "They just strip the bones out before they get it ready to fry."

"That's a pretty good idea," he replies like he can't wait to tell somebody else what a fillet is.

I'm making progress.

Next is Hibbett. I stop out front.

"Taiquon," I say. "If I was a college coach, and I bought you some stuff, it would be against the rules. On my side, there ain't nothing wrong with buying a kid some equipment to play baseball with. Now, I don't know the rules, 'cause I ain't never bought a kid nothing before, and it could be that the High School League would say it's wrong if anybody knew about it, but I never even heard about anything like that. I just think that, just in case, it might be best not to do much talking about it."

"Yes, sir."

"I might as well let you know. I know you don't have a glove of your own. Your coach told me. I know the reason you started catching is that every team you ever played for provided the catcher with a mitt. There's no reason for you to be embarrassed about that. It's just that I think a kid who might become a professional ballplayer ought to have some equipment of his own to use."

"Yes, sir."

"Where'd you get your cleats?" I ask.

"One of my teammates got some new ones and passed his down to me. Rashun Dixon."

"I notice they were taped up. I'll get you fitted for some new ones. You don't use a batting glove."

"No, sir," he says. "I don't think it makes no difference."

God. How refreshing.

I buy him some, though, and let him pick out some cleats, black with red trim because Vosbrinck wears those colors.

"If you were playing in the field, what you like playing better?" I ask. "Infield or outfield?"

He says outfield, as I expected he would.

"An outfielder wears a bigger glove than an infielder," I say. "When you are fielding the ball and throwing to first, you can't let it get lost in a big glove so you fumble with it a little."

I get him a twelve-incher, and it's on sale at not much over half price. I ask him if he wants to pick out a bat for himself, but he says, no, he's partial to one in the team bag. That's good because, if everything goes right, he's going to have to learn how to hit with wood pretty soon.

"Anything else?" I ask.

"No, sir," Taiquon says. "I sure 'preciate it."

The kid won't ask for a thing. May it forever be so.

When we get back to Grandma's house, Taiquon says she's working. I tell him again I want to meet her soon.

"When she sees this stuff I bought you, she's liable to think I'm a con man," I say. "I can tell I've got to earn her trust just like I've got to earn yours."

"I trust you."

"Don't say that," I reply. "You don't know me well enough yet. Anybody call you Ty?"

He's quiet for a moment.

"Grandma doesn't like nobody to call me nothing but Taiquon."

Taiquon it is. I watch him unlock the front door and see the lights turn on, then head back up the road toward Youngville. I have the two beers I've been craving at a little joint on Lake Bluefield. They've got a band playing, but I don't much care for it, and I don't see a soul I know, so I head on home a little after dark.

CHAPTER 8
A Cure for What Ails Me

━━⟆⟅━━

I'm feeling sorry for myself as I drive to Vosbrinck for the umpteenth time. I've been fueled by a desire to prove the ball club wrong. I want Taiquon Wattson to be my project. I want him to prove that I know a ballplayer when I see one, and I can see one no one else can. I can make a decision with my gut that the algorithms, analyses, and various and sundry other methods based purely on numbers cannot. That's the world. It's passed me by. I'm a dinosaur. I can still rule, though. I watched a *Jurassic Park* movie once. The back of my mind contains a nodule of self-doubt. I don't know whether or not realizing it exists is a blessing or a curse. When I was young, I could keep it suppressed. I didn't consciously know it was there. I was blissfully ignorant. Now, since I acknowledge its existence, I should be able to prosper from it. Reality provides no serenity. It can be a rainy day like this one. It's clearing out, though. The rain. Tonight's game between the Vosbrinck Chiefs and the Ware Shoals Hornets will be cool and misty if it's anything at all. I wish it was in Ware Shoals. It's a lot closer, and the Hornets play in this old textile stadium I once played in. Ware Shoals is a tiny place, but Riegel Stadium was built in the twenties or thirties, the twentieth century, and I still remember this old guy telling stories about big-league teams holding exhibition games there back in the day when men were men and worked in cotton mills.

But I digress. I'm not headed there. Vosbrinck's diamond isn't bad for the end of the earth.

I'm waxing nostalgic trying to cure the blues.

46

This time I'm not taking my scorebook. I've got a notepad crammed in my pocket. No pencils, just a couple of rollerball pens, one blue and one red. The day began with the usual mug of coffee as I watched a *Columbo* rerun. I didn't ever watch that show when Peter Falk was alive. Now I've seen every episode three times. Then I had a bowl of raisin bran because I just didn't feel like cooking, and that is unusual. The blues. Damn 'em. It's six when I reach the mild city traffic of Bluefield. It's still raining. The game will never start on time, if at all. I think about turning around. Instead, I go through a McDonald's for two road burgers – small cheeseburgers, not too messy to eat while driving – and a small Diet Dr. Pepper, not too large to make me have to pee at the game.

Apparently, it's just been drizzling all day. The annoying announcer is yelling the Vosbrinck lineup over the public address as I pay my way into the park with my foldout chair and a gym bag on my shoulders. Twenty-five people are here, besides the teams. I can't blame them too much for staying home. Unless the drizzle stops, the notepad is going to remain in my pocket. I can talk into my phone if I need to remind myself of something. Undoubtedly, I could talk my way into the press box. I could've talked my way into the game without paying five bucks. I just don't want any human interaction. Taiquon and Coach Torin Ferguson will notice I'm here. With this many fans, everyone here is going to notice everyone else. Ware Shoals goes up and down in order in the first. The Hornets' leadoff man must be no taller than five-foot-four. I'd sure take a strike if I was he. He tries to bunt on the first pitch, and Taiquon pounces on the ball and throws him out by ten feet. I want to see him throw from the outfield.

Taiquon has his new batting gloves when he bats in the first inning. He flies out to the medium center field. The Chiefs scratch out a run. It's the first time I've seen them score when he didn't have anything to do with it. The next time up, leading off the third, the gloves aren't on. Behind in the count, one and two, he hits a line drive that looks like it's going to bounce into the left-center gap for extra bases, only it keeps going, right out of the park. It never got more than fifteen yards off the ground. I couldn't believe how far it carried, even struck by an aluminum bat. That's when I noticed something I'd missed.

I call it a cantilevered swing, even though I looked up "cantilevered" in the dictionary once, and that's not what the swing is. It's like a football announcer saying a running back "matriculates" down the field. It's stupid, but it's colorful. I haven't ever seen but a few, and the only player I could name who has one now is Dustin Pedroia. Pedroia takes the same swing on every pitch. He just adjusts to the plane of the pitch with his legs. Few can do it, and now his legs are about gone. It's such a talent that most players would do well not to try. Taiquon Wattson has a cantilevered swing, and I can tell anyone I want because they won't know what it means, and they'll be right.

I no longer have the blues.

Vosbrinck leads, 7-4 going into the seventh (and final in high school ball) inning, when the little lefthander they've got on the mound suddenly can't find the plate. He walks the bases full on 13 pitches, only one of which is called a strike. None away. Clearly, something has to be done. Torin walks out to the mound with Taiquon's brand-new glove tucked under his armpits. He gives it to Taiquon and returns to the dugout carrying the mitt and catcher's gear. The pitcher can't catch because, not only is there no mitt for a lefthanded catcher in the equipment bag, but I have personally never seen one. The pitcher goes to first base, and the first baseman goes to catch. Taiquon obviously has to just throw the ball as hard as he can over the plate. By some small miracle, I've got a pair of binoculars in my little gym bag. I watch Taiquon warm up. He doesn't even put his fingers on the laces. He just grabs the ball the same way he would if he plucked it out of the dirt. He's on the money, though. Every pitch is around the plate. He strikes out the first batter. A run scores when the first-time catcher just whiffs at a pitch that's about chest-high. It hits the umpire right in the mask and knocks him so silly it's damned fortunate there wasn't a play at the plate.

Taiquon runs in and apologizes as if he had something to do with it. It takes three or four minutes for the ump to remember what state he's in.

Runners are on first and second, one out now. Taiquon finishes off the batter with a called third strike that the plate umpire somehow manages to call. The first pitch to the next batter is called a ball, even though it's right down the middle of the plate. The ump likely didn't see either one. The batter can't catch up to the next one but hits it like a shot down the right-field line. It sails over the fence, ten feet foul. He misses the pitch that ends the game by half a foot.

My late friend Dick Enberg would've said, "Oh, my." I say it to myself in his honor.

I hook up my earbuds to my phone on the way home after congratulating Taiquon and Torin, and I'm glad the stuff of legends has been witnessed by so few. I've never sat through a better night in the rain. I tell Taiquon to keep doing what he's doing and I'll be back in touch. I don't feel like I've got any business talking on a phone while I'm at the wheel on two-lane roads. As luck would have it, the phone rings, and it's Frank Staley Jr.

"How's your boy wonder?" Frank asks.

"I just saw the damnedest thing ever," I reply. "When I say that, I'm usually exaggerating. Not this time. It was seriously the damnedest thing I've ever seen. The kid went four for five, missed the cycle by a double, went out to the mound with bases loaded in the ninth, none away, and got a save the first time he ever pitched from a mound. Other'n'at, Taiquon wasn't no count."

"I take that to mean you still think this kid can play pro ball."

"Maybe not now," I said. "Frank, you've got to find me a place where he can play this summer. As long as it ain't Alaska, I might go with him. He needs work, but he's got the tools."

"Why not sign him to a free-agent contract and let him see what he can do in the instructional league?"

"One, he won't get any money to speak of out of the deal," I say. "Two, the only way he could be rawer would be if he was a sixteen-year-old from the Dominican. That's because the only advantage he's got is he already knows English."

"We've become quite enlightened over the years in bringing Latinos along," Frank says. "Hey, I thought you told me Taiquon didn't own a fielder's glove. Surely, he didn't go out on the mound with a mitt."

"I bought him a glove. That's what opened the door of opportunity for Taiquon to save the game."

"How can this kid possibly, in 2018, be this clueless? You sound like you found him pitching apples in a grove."

"Let me tell you something, Frank Staley Junior. Taiquon Watts doesn't have a cell phone. He's never played a video game. He doesn't have cable. He doesn't know what ESPN is. The networks don't televise a game of the week anymore. I doubt Taiquon even watched the World Series last fall because he was a big football star at the time. He only knows the NFL exists on Sundays. I bet he didn't know what the Portland Loggers were when I first told him I worked for 'em. You send him to Arizona when he graduates from high school, and he'll hitchhike home before the ink on the contract is dry. Find me somewhere in the middle of nowhere where he can play amateur summer ball, and give me the summer to make him worth a million bucks, and then you can sign him for a hundred grand."

In the back of my mind, where the self-doubt lurks, I know this isn't really why Frank Jr. called.

"I want you to take one more look at the Standback kid."

"My evaluation is well known," I say.

"I want you to do this for me, not the organization. The club's gonna take him with the third pick in the draft if I can't figure out a way to talk them out of it."

"I wouldn't take him with the thirty-third pick."

"I know you wouldn't, but you're big on intangibles. I want you to ask around again. Talk to the English teacher again. Use your celebrity. Talk to local folks about Standback who want to talk baseball with you. You know that drill."

"I do," I say. "One condition. If I sneak around and try to find a little more about this kid's character, you find me a place for my prospect to play."

Frank sighed.

"Deal."

CHAPTER 9
Just Add Water

Here I sit, brokenhearted. Tried to tell 'em. Disregarded.

Thought I was going to be nasty, didn't you? Untoward. Me? Never! I'm delighted I still have my sense of humor. The Portland Loggers have little regard for my proficiency in my chosen profession. One man, Frank Staley Jr., thinks I have value as a private investigator. I'm back in Haldeman, a skip and a jump from the warming spring waters of Lake Murray, mingling among the upscale clientele of what passes in these parts for a quirky coffee shop, wondering what's going on in the minds of a seventeen-year-old black kid and his stolid grandmother who live in quite different circumstances near the banks of another lake.

This other kid, Ryne Standback, might become a superstar. The major leagues certainly have their share of entitled brats who happen to have great talent. I just don't think he'll ever learn how to keep his personal ambitions in line with the goals of his team. That's the best case. Standback may burn out in the minors. He won't take to being humbled well. He hasn't faced but a handful of arms that will be commonplace in Lower A. When he fails, he won't blame himself. What this kid needs is a military school, not a fat contract.

All Standback has is a powerful swing. He doesn't know baseball. He knows that swing. He knows bodybuilding. His daddy's money has taught him all about them. My colleagues these days think that swing is all it takes. They think his family's money is a good influence. Standback has never been to the school of hard knocks before. Taiquon Wattson lives there.

All I can think of is one speck of common ground between these cases. I can read both of them. I know, from his bearing, that, however talented Ryne Standback is, he is also a bullshit artist. I can tell Taiquon isn't. The wrong one has the odds stacked against him.

One more thing I was right about. The English teacher just walked in the door. He stops by after school most days. I knew it. I looked at my notes before I left the house. Now I can't remember his name. It's the last name of a famous Hollywood director. Two, in fact. He's seen me and he's walking over. Sturges. John Sturges. Preston Sturges. This one isn't a director, though. He's a teacher, but his name fits him. William Sturges. Whew. He's here.

"Mister Kinlaw," he says.

"Mister Sturges," I reply.

"Would you like a refill?" he asks, glancing at my empty cup.

"Sure. Thank you."

"How about a nosh?" Sturges asks. What is a nosh? I guess I'll find out.

"Sure," I say.

"Let me select something for you," he says, turning toward the counter.

Undoubtedly, it's something to eat.

Sturges returns with a tray. He brings back my coffee and his, and two flaky pieces of pastry, coated with what looks like caramel or maple syrup and, most likely, almond shavings. I like nosh, it appears. Sturges said "a nosh," so these must be noshes.

"One last look at Ryne Standback?" Sturges asks.

"Yessir," I say.

"Call me Will. I take it your team – it's the Loggers, right? must be considering drafting Ryne in the first round."

"It's not on my recommendation ... Will ... but, yes, a friend in the organization asked me to take one more look and see what I could find out about him."

"He wasn't always such a brat, Ryne Standback. I had him in the ninth grade," Sturges says. "He just loved playing baseball. That's when scouts, pretty much college coaches, started paying attention. You know he always was the kind of kid who'd spent his whole life hearing everyone tell him how wonderful, how smart, he was. Kid started believing them."

I just listen.

"Three years later, I'm teaching him again. He's a totally different kid. He made an early commitment to the Gamecocks when he was fifteen. He couldn't even drive yet. He started hanging out with the seniors. It's been a year since I overheard Ryne talking about college, other than when every sportswriter at every game asks him about it, and he feeds them the same, standard line about thinking education is important, and it will be valuable preparation for a professional career. He doesn't care about his studies anymore. I'm satisfied every paper he turns in was written for him by someone else."

"Has a lot of writing styles, does he?"

"Many of them strangely feminine in tone," Sturges says. "Ryne cares about two things, money, and sex."

"I'm well acquainted with those temptations, Will."

"We all are, to one extent or another."

"If there's a difference," I say, "it's that I got what I got naturally. What talent I had, I came by it, naturally, not so much from weightlifting. I got it from working on the farm. I played different sports all year long and was good at all of them. I didn't lose a grip on my morals till I had the money, and the money brought the women. In other words, the difference between young Mister Standback and me at the same age is I never took a trip until I'd already left the farm."

Without further details, I take the last swallow of my second coffee and bid farewell to my willing spy Will Sturges. I twist around and find, in a box in the back seat, an old paperback of the book written in my name, *Baseball the Kinlaw Way,* twenty-five years ago.

I've still got boxes and boxes of them in the basement.

Quickly, I scrawl on the title page, between "by Clyde Kinlaw" and "as told to Harmon Jackson":

To William Sturges,
Just read this inscription. Don't read the book.
Clyde Kinlaw #8

I slide one of my business cards into the middle pages and hand it to him.

Sturges glances at what I signed.

"You were thirty-eight for the Sox," he says.

"They had this other famous number eight. Thanks for the info."

I never met Yaz. He was gone before I got there, and I didn't join the Red Sox until the end of spring training after he had already flown back to Long Island. It's the same way I fly home from Flagstaff now.

When I leave the lot, I notice that Sturges is following me. I'm driving aimlessly, looking for a place to kill a few hours. Preferably, it's a local place with a different clientele. In most towns, I'd look for a beer joint. A few might be over on the lake, but patrons there won't be reliably conversant with Haldeman. I reason that a wings bar is the best I can do, and I pull in when I find one with burnt-orange-stained wood and something of a switchback gangplank to stroll up in order to get inside. It looks like a hundred trendy others. Sturges drives on.

I park again, this time at the bar, and order a draught. Two unshaven fellows to my right seem to be talking inexplicably of religion. Trump may be involved and in a good way. I take a healthy swig from my glass mug. I bet it costs a place like this money if the mugs aren't frosty. Word gets around a town like this. For me, it's not a deal-breaker.

Tuning my ears' attention to the left finds two Gamecock fans who have decided Ray Tanner needs to come down out of that ivory tower known as athletics director and take that baseball team back to the College World Series. Recognizing that there is some interest in the national pastime, I don't turn toward them because it might encourage their recognition. These two are from the generation that might remember me. I finish my first rather quickly, order another, wait for it, pay the youthful barkeep, and take the new and again frosty mug to a booth with me, resigned to the reality that no intelligence-gathering will occur here.

I like the beer, though. I might not even go inside the gate. I might be able to park the truck out beyond the fence. That way I can train my binoculars on Ryne Standback and watch his interactions, and his body language. I need something specific, some character flaw other than me thinking he's a self-centered brat who's going to take an absurdly predictable fall. I told Frank Junior I'd take one more look at him. I didn't say it would do any good. Besides, if I watch the game from the truck, I might sip a few more beers.

I hear a lovely voice.

"You are Clyde Kinlaw?"

I see a lovely woman. The eight or nine others in the place see her, too. She could be the woman of my dreams but probably isn't because I've seen such women twice before with disastrous results. This woman is about forty, which is great because she maintains a graceful, healthy beauty. I bet she plays tennis, particularly since her clothes suggest she just got finished. Her perfume is affected by an afternoon sweat. It may have been designed for that. I find it appealing and finish my second beer. I realize I've not yet replied.

"Uh, yes. And you are?"

"Drema. Drema McLeod. May I sit down?"

"Please do," I say, and, as she swings her handbag to her side and slides into the booth, I finish my second beer.

The waitress who arrives is cute, but I find her lacking when I project twenty years from now at Drema's approximate age. My attention might be unseemly to the girl because she doesn't know the gist of my thoughts. No. I think she's mildly flattered. A man my age can flirt without as much risk because both parties realize the absurdity of the notion. Does one have to speak to flirt?

Drema orders a bottled Heineken for herself and a refill of whatever I am drinking. The girl asks me what I am drinking.

"Ask the bartender," I say. "It's on special."

"Do you have an appetizer platter?" Drema asks the waitress.

"Yes, it comes with ..."

"I don't mean to be impolite, Phyllis, but it doesn't matter. Mister Kinlaw and I just need something to munch on while we're discussing a private matter."

"Sure thing, Mrs. McLeod. I'll put 'em in pronto."

Drema sighs and shakes her head. "Phyllis should be in college," she says. "I guess she must have dropped out again."

I can think of no need for a response. I fold my arms on the table and wait expectantly.

The beers arrive. Drema hands Phyllis a five as a tip and says run a tab.

"I'm thirsty," she says to me. "I expect I'll have two."

"What's on your mind?" I finally ask.

"My guess, Clyde, is that you are in Haldeman to take one more look at Ryne Standback, our local sporting hero."

"Lest you think I'm drinking on the job, Mrs. McLeod..."

"Oh, please," she says. "Call me Drema. I'm going to call you Clyde."

"Drema, what I came down here to do is ask around and see what kind of kid Standback is off the field. His talent is going to make him a lot of money, but whichever team shells out the kind of money he's going to get is going to want some assurance that he's got some character."

"I saw you earlier in the season," she says. "While all the other scouts were practically mobbing Ryne, you were detached. I got the notion that you were not impressed with him."

"To Standback's great benefit, others in my organization do not think much of my evaluations," I say. "There may be one guy in the front office who doesn't think I'm past my prime, and he asked me to take one more look around and see if I can confirm my suspicions about the lad."

"Clyde, this is your lucky day," she says.

"I take it you and Will Sturges are well acquainted," I say.

"Yes, but why?"

"Will told you this is where I was."

Drema's look is neutral.

"He followed me here from the coffee shop," I say. "When I turned in, he kept going. He wanted to know where I was."

"Aren't you the detective?" Her expression suggests she likes this.

"Mister Sturges isn't exactly a trained spy," I say. "I probably went around in several circles trying to pick out a place like this to hang out. If you hadn't snuck in, I'd have nothing. Now, what is it you have to tell me about Ryne Standberg?"

"His girlfriend of the moment is my daughter," she says.

"Oh?"

"Since Christmas. He's had a bad effect on her. I'm worried as a mother."

"Forgive my frankness, Drema, but we *are* drinking beer here. Is he using a condom?"

I almost cause a spit take, but Drema regains her composure quickly.

"Disney used to be wholesome. The American Dream."

"Excuse me?"

"Disney. My daughter."

"Oh," I say. "I thought you meant Disney like in the movies."

Drema realizes what she said and laughs merrily. My innards tingle.

"I'm definitely going to have another beer," she says.

"Me, too," I say, and that will be four.

"Disney's attitude turned bad. She thinks everything is bullshit."

"When, in fact, we adults know that no more than three-quarters of it is," I say.

"She started smoking. I don't think cigarettes is all."

"Any evidence?" I ask.

"Not her. Late one Friday night after a game, Ryne and three other starters on the team got busted over on the lake," Drema says.

"That's interesting."

"There's no proof. The charges got dropped, of course. They're athletes. Ryne is getting national publicity for how much money he's going to get in the baseball draft. Most folks don't want to mess it up for him."

I'm ready for a fifth draught. Drema orders a third Heineken. She keeps up pretty well. A few post-match beers are not unfamiliar to her, I'd wager.

When the order arrives, Drema says, "Phyllis?"

"Yes, ma'am?"

"Mister Kinlaw is a professional baseball scout. He's here to watch Ryne Standback play tonight. We are acquaintances," Drema lies. "I don't want you to get the wrong impression."

"Oh, no. 'Course not." Phyllis retreats, looking as if she's ready for a smoke break.

We talk about baseball for a while. I expect it bores her. Finally, I drift back to the subject at hand.

"It's not unusual for an early-round draft pick to test positive for marijuana," I say. "When I was a kid, I drank sometimes while I was underage. It was easier to get back then. One reason so many kids smoke pot now is that it's so easy to get. Weed dealer never asks for I.D."

"What happens?"

"Well, once they're under contract, the scout advises a kid to be honest, says it won't affect anything, but if there's any chance he's gonna flunk a drug test, say so. If that's the case, the club keeps him in extended spring training until they think he's clean, and he really doesn't get to play on an honest-to-God, traveling team, you know, for a full season, until the following year. At eighteen years of age, he's got plenty of time. A college kid is more reliable because they've been through drug testing there."

"Disney is supposed to enroll at Carolina in the fall," Drema says. "I think she's planning to run away with Ryne Standback and his million-dollar bonus."

"It's way more than that," I say.

"He's telling everybody ten million dollars."

"Not that much," I say, "at least not if he thinks my club is going to pick him. I'm here because that's the plan, and that means they have come pretty close to getting a contract negotiated right now."

"Did you recommend it?" she asks.

"I did not."

"I didn't think so."

"I told you they don't listen to me," I say.

"Tell your friend in the front office not to do it," she says. "Ryne Standback is going to get busted again, and this time it's going to stick."

"I take it you have inside information."

"My husband's brother is a state senator," Drema says. "Before he was state senator, Fred was the solicitor. His chief assistant has the job now. Fred knows a lot of people in law enforcement."

"Fred McLeod, huh? He'll do this for you?"

"He'll do it for Jack. Jack's my husband."

"Huh, your husband was a big star at Carolina, right?"

"I was the homecoming queen," she says.

"I am absolutely sure you were," I say, "and I'm not too sure you wouldn't win it right now."

"That's sweet," Drema says. "I like you."

"I like you, too, Drema, but if this kid Standback's as much of a shit as you think he is, he'll leave your daughter behind. She'll be back home by the Fourth of July."

"If I knew you were right, Clyde ... I'd still have him arrested."

"If that kid has any sense, Drema, he won't cross you."

"Oh, the kids in town all think I'm the coolest," she says.

I'm not sure whether I'm drunk or just taken aback, but by the time I get to the ballfield, the Haldeman Eagles are already up, 7-0, and some fans are leaving at the end of the third inning. It is thus easy for me to slide into a spot next to the fence down the left-field line. A drive would have to carry a long way foul for it to hit the truck. Rather than a six-pack, I bought myself a small vat of coffee on the way. I rummage around behind the seat and find my camera. I switch the setting to where it freezes the shake in faraway shots, and I snap a few shots of Standback goofing around in the dugout and holding a runner at first. He hits a homer in the fifth, but I don't get a picture of it because I'm screened by the third-base coach. He's a pure hitter who plays first base because it's comparatively easy. It's not easy to be good at it, though, and he isn't. His arm is strong. He's built like a baby bull. He runs well. At this level, Ryne does just about whatever he wants.

What have I got against Ryne Standback? A disgruntled English teacher. A concerned mother. Drug allegations. I've got nothing to dissuade people who possess all-seeing, all-knowing numbers. I try not to care. I sit a while, though, ruminating about my adventures, and a big, white, jacked-up, four-wheel-drive Toyota pickup roars by. Standback owns this vehicle. It's exactly the vehicle he owns. Teammates are crammed inside, leaning out the windows, and sitting in the bed. They are not going to Bible study.

I pull out quickly and follow for a while, but they head out into the country somewhere. I'm not particularly tired, though, and I'm hungry again, as much thirsty for beer, truthfully, but I could use a burger. Then I think, well, I haven't actually had those wings, so I head back there. Nobody notices me. It's Friday night, and some rowdy kids are home from school for the weekend, showing off their recent acquisition of the right to buy beer and drink it right out in public. The conquering heroes of the diamond charge into great hurrahs at about the time my wings, garlic and parmesan, arrive with the second beer of my second visit. Phyllis is still working. It's probably good she sees me here again, alone, because people who say they won't talk are prone to lie, so she knows that, in all likelihood, Mrs. McLeod and I are not secret lovers. I wolf down my wings hurriedly and reward Phyllis handsomely. I time my exit to just when a major rock anthem starts to blare, but I don't believe Ryne Standback has any memory of meeting me a month ago now. It's all a blur now. He and his buddies do not appear sober.

I move my truck to a location that leaves me a clear field of vision to Standback's four-by-four and waits. They're on rendezvous with their girlfriends, who were waiting for them at the wings joint. Several couples come outside to stand around and sit on the tailgate. Standback is the last to emerge, likely having been slowed by the acknowledgment of his celebrity inside. Disney McLeod is the image of her mother, but she is not quite as statuesque, and her hair is unnaturally blonde. Standback tells a kid to get off his tailgate so there's room for him and Disney, who is sucking on a compact apparatus and then exhaling a cloud that quickly dissipates. Standback has one, too, and I know he and his buds have gone somewhere to burn weed before they got here, and now they're smoking vapor, or, I think, this must be what they call "vaping." For all I know, there might be a way to suck pot through these things. I've seen these e-cigarettes, shaped like regular ones but tipped with a blue light that glows when they "hit" them. My cell has wi-fi, so I google "vaping" and, from the pictures, determine these vaping devices must be "juuls." Apparently, they are quite the rage with the young crowd.

Meanwhile, I'm clicking away at all this, and now I have something. In this day and age, the Portland scouting department might fret more about tobacco than cannabis.

When I was in the minors, we'd have four or five guys who smoked cigarettes in the locker room, and I know of at least one who smoked pot in the bullpen john.

CHAPTER 10

Mama's Okay

The wi-fi at the house, meanwhile, is out, and I haven't got time to deal with it. I'm spending another Saturday afternoon with Taiquon Wattson. I'm picking him up again when he gets off work at the Food Lion in Vosbrinck. I've got to talk with Frank Staley Jr. about my latest Ryne Standback report. The library is too quiet a place to conduct an animated phone conversion, so I go to McDonald's to use the free Internet there. It's prime breakfast time when I get there, but I realize that the bulk of the business is in the drive-through nowadays because the dining area is sparsely occupied. Perfect. I slide into a booth, set up my laptop, and get up to order a coffee. McDonald's stresses the quality of its coffee. It sells its brand in supermarkets. Maybe I don't know what good coffee tastes like. This tastes like hot muddy water to my palate. I wish I'd brought my own. I paid for it. I'll drink it.

It's a wonderland of beeping noises. I guess they're going off because the hash browns are ready to hoist out of the deep fryer, the latest pot of coffee is hot, and no telling what else. As far as I know, there may be a beeper to tell Kathy it's time for her break, so she can now step outside to smoke, or, maybe, "juul." It sounds like a bunch of golf carts are backing up. I see there's an email from Frank Junior but don't open it yet. I go back to the counter and order the last two cookies, one chocolate chip, and the other oatmeal raisin, from the display. The sturdy but pretty redhead, the one I have imagined as Kathy, drops the oatmeal raisin on the floor. I tell her I'll take just the chocolate chip, then. It doesn't make much difference as I'll be washing it down with muddy water.

I open the email.

Clyde,

I see you have officially submitted a glowing report regarding our No. 1 draft pick. I suspect a method in your madness. Call me. – FSJ.

I call. He's expecting me and answers on the first ring.

"Clyde," he says. "Who are you? Sherlock Holmes?"

"I take it you have reviewed the private report I sent you."

"Where in the hell did you get all that information?" he asks.

"Uh, I just hung out in town. The English teacher, Sturges, I met the first time I went down there. I thought I might catch him at the same coffee shop I stopped by before, and I was right. William is something of a regular there after school."

"And the woman?"

"She looked me up," I reply. "I reckon you could say William Sturges and Drema McLeod are in cahoots. When I left the coffee shop, I noticed Sturges following me. I pulled in at a wing joint, and Mrs. McLeod showed up a few minutes later."

"And they don't care much for Ryne Standback."

"They don't like him worth a damn."

"Why might that be?" Frank Junior asks.

"Well," I say, "Drema's good-looking daughter is seeing young Mister Standback, and, by the way, you're not gonna believe what the young woman's first name is."

"Go ahead. Tell me."

"Disney," I say. "Disney McLeod."

"I'll be damned," Frank says.

"That's what Drema says Mister Standback is doing to her daughter. Her attitude stinks. She started smoking. Her mother thinks it's more than cigarettes. Her mother wants her at the

University of South Carolina next fall. Drema thinks she's going to run off with Ryne as soon as he signs for the big bucks."

"And the photos?"

"That was pure luck, Frank. When the game was over, I was hungry, so I headed back to the wings joint to have a dozen hot ones and a couple of beers. When I left the ballyard, the Standback kid passed me with a pile of his teammates whooping and hollering in the back of his four-wheel-drive. I followed them away. I figured they were going out to the lake to celebrate, so I went on over to the wings joint. I was just about done when Standback and his buddies rolled in. Disney and a bunch of other girls were waiting for them. I finished off the wings, ordered another beer, and just kept tabs on them idly. Finally, I paid the bill and walked outside. I moved my truck to where I had a view of Standback's pickup, and a few minutes later, they all tumbled outside to hang out around it."

"That's where you took the pictures of Standback and his girlfriend using the Juuls?"

"If I was a betting man," I say, "I'd put my money on them ballplayers going out in the country to smoke weed, and that's why they were craving cigarettes when they met their girlfriends. I expect getting stoned to be kind of a bonding deal for the ballplayers. I didn't even know what a Juul was. I'm surprised you do."

"You're unbelievable," Frank says. "You really could be a detective."

"I watch old episodes of *Columbo* a lot," I say.

"Did you use marijuana when you were playing, Clyde?"

"Everybody used drugs when I was playing, Frank. When I started out, players took amphetamines, 'greenies,' they called them, to keep their energy up from playing games day after day and night after night. I never did. I drank a lot of beers late at night, and I smoked a little pot from time to time. By the time I reached the bigs, lots of players were snorting coke instead of popping pills. I never did any of that, but I'm not pure as the driven snow, either. Let's just say I know enough to know it when I see it. For what it's worth, my guess is that Drema McLeod does, too. She's well-connected. Prominent family. I think she studied who I was for a while before she tracked me down. She made note of me when I scouted Standback the first time and filed it away because she could tell I wasn't as impressed as the rest were. I believe she wants me to wreck Ryne Standback, and, if I don't, which I'm not, she's gonna wreck him herself. She told me that."

"You believe her, Lieutenant Columbo?"

"I do, Frank. I do. Don't draft that brat. Sign the best arm. Take a pitcher. It's cheaper and less risky."

"I've heard you say that before," Frank says, "and I've always meant to ask you what you mean. You weren't a pitcher. Why come you're in favor of making them the majority of a team's draft choices?"

"Because," I say, "position players are less risky. Pick pitchers and develop them yourself. If one of 'em's arm goes bad, you wasted less money. Use your free-agent money on position players. They're much more likely to put up numbers for the length of the contract. You sign the best pitcher in the league to an eight-year contract, and he may be washed up before the end of his first year. It happens all the time. I can't understand why nobody ever seems to notice. Matter of fact, Frank, sign a high school pitcher so that you can develop and take care of him yourself. Lots of college coaches will ruin a kid's arm in order to win ballgames."

"You're gonna have me crunching numbers on those notions for the rest of the day," Frank says.

"About time," I reply. "Look, you asked me to do something. I did it. I'm headed off to Vosbrinck right now to learn more about Taiquon Wattson. The high-school season is winding down. Now you find me a place where he can play, and I can make him into a ballplayer. I'm making plans, Frank. Have team, will travel."

"I'm on it, Clyde. By the way, I caught my daughter with a Juul last week."

"I'm sorry to hear that."

That explains why Frank Junior and I now know what a Juul is.

Back on the road, I feel rotten. I don't like dealing with Ryne Standback, and I don't like being a hypocrite, either. In the short run, I'm confident Standback is going to be a bust. The first time he's somewhere, all alone, in a place where he doesn't feel nearly as important, he's going to blame every problem he's got on someone other than himself. He may grow up. I did. I wasn't as entitled at his age, but, when the amount of my income roared right past the amount of my maturity, I made some mistakes for which I am still paying. For twenty years, I paid for those mistakes with my wallet. Now I pay for them with a leak in my soul.

I reckon I call Torin Ferguson because I want to stop thinking about Ryne Standback. The Chiefs have earned a number-two regional seed in the playoffs. That means a first-round home game on Wednesday. Taiquon has been selected to play in something called the Extra-Grip North-South All-Star Game in late May after the playoffs are over. If Vosbrinck makes it to the state championship game in Class Double-A, then Taiquon won't get to participate.

Vosbrinck is not going to the state finals. Taiquon won't get them there if he bats a thousand. The more exposure he gets, the more the chance my secret gets out. It's unavoidable. It's astonishing I've made it this far.

"Great news, Torin. I'm happy for Taiquon, too."

"You think you might be getting some competition for him?" Torin asks.

"I'm surprised it hasn't happened before now. He's got to make his own decisions. I hope he'll be grateful for what I'm trying to do, but he's got to do what's best for him and his mama."

"He's a great kid. He'll stick with you. I'll talk to him."

"Torin, when I say this, I'm not sure you'll believe it, and, if the roles were reversed, I might not believe it from you. I want something from Taiquon, but it's not money. I might make some, but it won't be worth everything I put into this. In my business, most people think the world has passed me by. I'm living in yesterday. What I want from Taiquon is a chance to prove them wrong. I'm not really working for the organization. I'm in contact with Portland. What work I do, though, is going to be for Taiquon. I really don't honestly know yet whether he's got what it takes. I think he might. I think I might be able to get him there. He's got the talent, and he can develop the skills, but that doesn't mean he's going to make it. I think I can get him his shot, and I won't let him take it unless or until I know he's got a decent shot."

"I believe you, Clyde."

"I appreciate that, Torin, but you're his coach, not mine. Don't close any doors for him, but don't open 'em wide open, either."

"I hear you," Torin says.

Taiquon's smile is more than the usual bright when he climbs into the truck. He must know about making the all-star team. I ask him where we can go talk where there's some privacy. I'm aware that, if we go over to his house, the presence of my truck parked out front, and the rumor that a white man drives it, will create a certain neighborhood commotion. Taiquon knows it, too.

"I doubt there's nobody out at Stackhouse Creek," he says.

Stackhouse Creek State Park lies on the banks of Lake Thurmond a few miles west of town. We eschew the lakefront pavilion and stop at a shaded picnic shelter. I've got a small cooler that I took the liberty of loading with Mountain Dews for Taiquon and Diet Dr. Peppers for me.

"What I thought, when I first decided you might have a chance to make it in baseball," I say, "is that I might work you out on Saturdays. I changed my mind because, right now, you gotta worry about your team, and I don't want to interfere with Coach Ferguson."

"Yes, sir."

"You need to get your rest. If Coach wants you to have a workout on Saturday, that's his business, but it ain't my business. I'm trying to make arrangements, once school is out, for you to play somewhere. I don't know where yet, but I'm gonna go with you. I might be your coach. I want to make sure you get what you need to be ready for pro ball."

"Yes, sir."

"You're good with that?" I ask.

"Yes, sir."

"What about your mama?"

"Well, I ain't talked to her about it much yet."

"What do you think?"

"I think she wants what's best for me," he says.

"You want me to talk to her?"

"Yes, sir."

If I keep asking yes-and-no questions, there's no telling what he'll say "yes, sir" to.

"I haven't got anything yet," I say. "I've got a friend trying to find a league, a team, something out there somewhere that might work. What I've got in mind is a summertime league that runs, maybe, from June the fifteenth to August the first. Six or seven weeks. I think that might be how much time you need."

"Yes, sir."

"There are areas where you need work," I say. "Things you don't do 'cause you don't know to do 'em. When you're behind the plate, you need to learn how to shift your body and not just lunge with your backhand to block balls in the dirt. You need to learn to hop around back there."

"Yes, sir," he says. It's his three-and-oh, automatic-strike call.

For about an hour, I lecture him about baserunning mistakes I've seen him make. I explain how he doesn't need to pull up at first when he singles in a run from second. If the throw goes through, and he takes second, he's in scoring position. If the other team cuts it and makes a play at second, even if he gets thrown out, the run scores and the odds are he'll be safe.

"Coach Treadway holds me up," he says.

"I know, and I want you to do what he says," I reply, "but I want you to know what to do when you ain't playing here no more. If I'm your coach, I'm gonna want you to make those plays."

"Yes, sir."

"At practice, has Coach Ferguson got you working on your pitching?"

"Now he does."

"That's good. You might come in handy pitching in the playoffs. Have you practiced throwing a curve?"

"No, sir." At last, a no. "Just fastball and a little less fastball."

I laugh. "I think that'll pass for a change-up. Have you ever heard of a cut fastball?"

"No, sir."

"It just puts a little break on your fastball." I reach into my bag and pull out a ball. "You throw with two fingers across the seams, don't you?"

I hold the ball up, with my index and middle fingers grasping the laces. "Like that," I say.

"Yes, sir."

"Okay, then. What I want you to try in practice on Monday is by holding the ball off-center. Take your middle finger and put it straight across the laces," I say, demonstrating, "then turn your index finger down to the left. You're shifting both fingers. Now throw it exactly the same as if your fingers weren't like that. Just throw the fastball with your fingers turned left. I believe you can adjust to that without much practice."

"You think I could be a pitcher?" he asks.

"No, I don't. I think you've got a live arm. I just know you're going to pitch a little in these playoffs, and I think that'll help you. Is the backup catcher getting any better?"

"A little," Taiquon says.

"Practice it with him. It's not gonna look like a lollipop curve," I say. "It's just gonna bend to the left a little at the plate."

We talk baseball for ten or fifteen minutes more. Well, I talk baseball, and Taiquon says "yes, sir," a lot, but it's better than having some kid tell me to mind my own business. Ryne Standback would do that.

When we arrive back at Taiquon's, a white Olds Achieva is parked out front.

"Are you responsible for keeping your grandmama's car clean and shiny?" I ask.

Taiquon doesn't say anything.

"That is her car?"

"Yes, sir."

"Well, don't you reckon it's about time for me to meet her?" I ask.

"Yes, sir." He seems a tad reluctant.

I imagine a stern woman. I'm not looking forward to this, either. I've got to convince this woman that I've got the best interests of her grandson in mind. I figure I've got a sales job to do, and it's not going to work if I act like it's a used car I've got to sell. Taiquon is a good kid, but he's naive and innocent.

I've gotten to know him well enough to realize it's not an act. Vosbrinck is a remote, safe harbor from the world around it. It's not that way for everyone who lives here. There's a satellite dish on the roof of the house next door.

It's Taiquon's house, but he doesn't just walk right in. We get to the front door, and he stops. He seems content just to stand there. I ring the doorbell, not knowing what else to do

When Ophelia Sanders opens the door, and I introduce myself, I could scarcely be more surprised. I'm expecting an Ophelia; it fits the image in my mind. The woman named Ophelia does not. She has the practical fashion sense of a woman who buys her clothes at yard sales, and no one knows it. She is attractive. I was expecting someone older, but then I do some math in my mind and realize that, if Taiquon's mother was born when Mrs. Sanders was eighteen, and his mother had him when she was eighteen, the grandmother could be my age. She looks younger.

I haven't found anyone I don't like in Vosbrinck. I like Torin Ferguson. I like Helen Bauer, the principal. I worry that Ophelia won't like me, mainly because Taiquon has seemed reluctant for me to meet her. I want to take her grandson away. Her house is neat and comfortable. A portrait of Obama is on the wall, and it takes me back to when I was a teen-ager, and the homes of my black friends had portraits of Martin Luther King and Jack Kennedy on the walls.

"Mr. Kinlaw, I understand you think my grandson has the potential to pay major league baseball," she says, inviting me to have a seat on the couch under Obama's gaze.

"I think he's got a shot, Mrs. Sanders," I say.

She says to call her Ophelia. I tell her I'm Clyde. She asks if I have any plans for supper. I say I was wondering the same thing and would like to take her and Taiquon out somewhere.

"I'm sort of tired, Clyde. It's been a long day. I can make some sandwiches."

"Do you and Taiquon like pizza?" I ask. "Maybe we can order out."

"I tell you what," she says. "Taiquon can go pick it up. That gives us a chance to talk."

If Taiquon has a driver's license, I am unaware. Before I can toss him the keys to my truck, Ophelia says he can go pick up the pizza on his bicycle.

"He walked to the Food Lion today because he knew you were picking him up," she says.

Taiquon is ahead of her. We walk out on the porch. I haven't seen a bike like that since I was in high school. It's an old Western Flyer with a basket on the front and headlights. Apparently, Western Auto built those things to last. It's got a little rust but looks well-oiled and reliable.

"How do you like your pizza, Clyde?" she asks.

"Ain't nothing you can put on a pizza I don't eat," I say.

Ophelia and I turns to Taiquon. "Get us a large, with sausage, mushrooms, pepperoni," she says. "Just order it at the front and wait for it. That way we know it'll be good and fresh."

She tries to give him some money, but I insist it's my treat.

The sun is setting. Ophelia and sit in rocking chairs and watch Taiquon pedal away. It's pleasant. Crickets chirp. People stroll by on the sidewalk. I feel like I have gone back to another place and time.

"Taiquon doesn't know much about the world," Ophelia says quietly.

"I know it," I reply. "I don't believe he's ready to go off on his own. He's got a lot to learn about baseball. I've got a lot to show him. I've been there. I've ridden in buses and lived with three other ballplayers in a cheap motel room made for one. I wasn't ready. I was readier than Taiquon is, but I wasn't, by no means, ready."

"You made it?"

"Yep," I say. "Somehow, some way."

"What happens if he signs with a ball team?" Ophelia asks. "What happens when you let him loose?"

I sigh. "If you'll trust me, that ain't the way it's gonna be for a good while. I don't think Taiquon needs to sign a contract now. I'm trying to find a place he can play, a place where I can watch him, work with him, and teach him things he needs to know. I don't want the pro ball to chew him up and spit him out. My plan is to stay with him as long as he needs it."

"And why would you be willing to do this, Clyde?"

"Well, Ophelia, I'm not a rich man. I ought to be. I got enough money coming in, though, from my big-league pension, that I'm fairly comfortable. I took a leave of absence from scouting. I'm not working with the big club right now. I don't expect Taiquon is going to make me rich. I want to make Taiquon a big-league ballplayer to show I can. I love your boy, Ophelia. He's like a gold nugget in a mountain stream. It won't do any good unless somebody finds it. Baseball's done got so high-tech and complicated that folks don't believe a kid like Taiquon exists anymore. I didn't believe it myself till I saw him. I got sent to scout another player. Taiquon grabbed my attention. There were a half dozen other scouts there. None of them noticed him 'cause wasn't anybody paying attention. They were all doing what I was supposed to do, which was to watch a big-time prospect name Ryne Standback. If I was in it for the money, that's who I'd be latching onto."

She digests that for a while and doesn't say anything.

Finally, I say, "What I want to know is can you do without him?"

"Sht," she says. She leaves out the 'i.' That way it isn't technically cussing. "I'll be fine, Clyde. Without Taiquon's mouth to feed, I'm liable to get right prosperous. I'll miss him. He's a good boy, but he doesn't need to get himself trapped in this town."

"I know he's a good boy, Ophelia. That wasn't the first thing I noticed. The first thing I noticed was his all-around athletic ability. It didn't take me long to get sold on what a good boy he really is, and I put a right good bit of effort into it."

"You have my blessing," she said.

I think to myself that it sounds like I'm asking for his hand in marriage.

Taiquon returns. He made sure he spent the twenty-five bucks I sent with him. He's got a two-liter bottle of Dr. Pepper and some bread sticks along with a huge, thick-crusted, square pizza. I believe it is called Sicilian. It's right tasty.

For the first time, I feel with confidence that Taiquon is on his way. I don't know where he's going, but I'm headed there, too.

CHAPTER 11

He Can't Say I Didn't Tell Him So

I'm in luck when I stop by Crosley's Office Supply because Dub Whatley is there, and I tell him about Taiquon Wattson and my attempts, thus far unsuccessful, to find a place for him to play and me to work with him this summer.

"He's eligible for Legion ball, ain't he?" Dub asks.

"I thought about that," I say. "Closest teams in Bluefield, but Taiquon's never played because, even though his grandmother's got a car, she's got nowhere near the time to take him, and I reckon don't none of his teammates play, and Taiquon's a great athlete, but I don't think it's reasonable to expect him to pedal an old Western Flyer bicycle to Bluefield and back. You know, Dub, he's one of those kids who ain't known as nothing but a great athlete. He plays whatever ball everybody else in town is playing. I don't think anybody really saw him as a baseball player till I come along. If he could get into college, they tell me he'd be headed off to play football or basketball. They know he's good at baseball, but, hell, that kid's good at everything but book learning. He ain't dumb by no means. He just ain't educated."

"Let he without sin cast the first stone," Dub says.

"I hear you," I say. "I was naïve when I signed a baseball contract, and it took a long time for trial and error to knock some sense into my head, but Taiquon's got so much coming from the school of hard knocks that he's liable not to recover. That's why he needs me to bring him along."

"Like a baseball version of *Pygmalion*," Dub says.

"That's the same as *My Fair Lady*, ain't it?"

"Just not a musical."

"Both of us just play dumb, you know it?"

"That's the South," Dub replies.

"How about them travel teams I keep hearing about?" I ask.

"I think they gotta be sixteen and under to play."

"There went that," I say. "I told Frank Staley Jr., my best contact with the Loggers, I'd go with Taiquon wherever he can find me some kind of summer team. He's looking. I reckon I'll just have to wait and see what he comes up with. Frank's busy with the draft right now. Taiquon ain't ready for the pro ball just yet. I believe Frank would sign him to a free-agent contract on my recommendation, but the boy needs some work before he's ready for that. Send him off to instructional league right now, and it would eat him alive. What I aim to do is get him good and ready 'fore I get Frank to watch me work him out."

"You really think a lot of him, don't you?"

"He's a great kid," I say. "He's got what the scouts call five tools. He can run, throw, field, hit, and hit with power. He's got no idea how good he is. I need to teach him fundamentals and build up his confidence. The best thing he's got going for him is he has no idea that he's got the ability to be somebody. Most kids the club sends me out to look at have been told by everybody how great they are, and, gradually, they've started believing it. Taiquon's got the tools without the ego. Most of 'em's got the ego without the tools."

I walk up the street and drop in to see Jimmy Daggett, my lawyer, and agent back when I needed one, but his secretary, after telling me how glad she is to see me, says Lawyer Daggett's in court and asks me if I want to give her a message.

"Nah," I say. "Nothing urgent. I'll catch him here directly."

I just need to see if Jimmy's got time to do some contract writing for me. I'm way ahead of myself on that.

I have this habit of making important decisions quickly and agonizing over things that are insignificant. For instance, right now, as I head down Interstate 26 toward Columbia, I'm considering my toaster. One of the elements is out, which means that this morning, the bagels just got toasted on one side. It doesn't make much difference. I might just keep using it till the other element, the one that apparently operates the outside of the two slots, fails. Or I could stop by Fred's and buy another cheap toaster similar to the one I got. If everything goes well, the state of my toaster won't make much difference because I'll be rooming with Taiquon in God knows where.

I'm going to Lexington to watch the Extra Grip North-South All-Star Game, not so much to offer Taiquon my support as to clear my conscience. I don't care for Ryne Standback, and I still don't think the Loggers should draft him in the first round. One skill a player has to learn is the knack for getting good wood on the ball. Aluminum bats yield lots of bloop hits that wouldn't occur if taking a rip at an inside pitch had the result it should have, which is to shear a bat in two. The college has many benefits, though. One is the small matter of education, but if a prospect is going to college just to play ball and not to learn about business administration or psychology, he's better off in the minors. My view is undoubtedly jaded by the fact that it was my path to the bigs. I do think dilly-dallying with a big-time college is good for a bargaining position. A kid like Standback is likely going to get more money if he's got a scholarship offer from Clemson, South Carolina, Florida, Vanderbilt – some college powerhouse – in his back pocket. A kid from these parts didn't get drafted until the end of the second round, and he got about twice the normal bonus – a million bucks, as I recall – because he was committed to Florida State, and the club that drafted him, the Yankees, had plenty of money to throw around.

As far as Standback is concerned, though, I feel a little guilty about knowing he's got an angry mama with a powerful husband trying to ruin him because he is screwing and otherwise corrupting their good-looking daughter. The kid's hardheaded.

I doubt he'll listen to me, but I need to at least tell him to watch his ass. The draft is in a couple of weeks. I don't want to see him ruined right at the point where's going to have a bundle of cash thrown at him. I don't want to see him sign with the Gamecocks just because it becomes his only option. I don't want to see Portland draft him, either, but, hell, I was a damned fool when I was his age, too. I'm almost positive warning him won't do any good, but maybe I'll sleep better tonight.

Lexington County Baseball Stadium is nicer than most of the minor league ballparks I played in. It's new and clean. It's short, 302 feet down the right-field line, and not too deep to left. The center is slightly under four hundred feet. It's a hitter's ballpark for pros, but probably just about right for high school. A summer college team, the Lexington County Blowfish, plays there. It's a wooden-bat league, and I'd love to get Taiquon a gig, but he's not in college and isn't going there. Collegiate leagues are everywhere. Decent semi-pro or amateur leagues? Not so much. I suppose there's good and bad in that. Maybe I can hook up with a team and coach first base or something.

I make my way down to the field as the North team is taking batting practice. I know all I need to know about Taiquon, but I don't want him to think I'm ignoring him because he's probably uptight already. I chat with him and tell a few jokes, trying to loosen him up by making him laugh.

Standback holds court, blasting pitch after pitch in batting practice. Whoever heard of flipping his bat in the batting cage? Taiquon blasts just as many, but most of them are rockets to the gaps. His home runs just clear the fences by fifteen feet, not fifteen miles. Taiquon's the one who acts like he's been here before. He's got a lot of disadvantages. He's clueless in many ways, but his grandma's raised him right, and Standback's parents treat him like he's their meal ticket. At some point, they'll remind him of all they've done for him, and he'll stop speaking to them and cut them off. I hope they get an Escalade out of the deal first. If that kid makes the big leagues, Haldeman will never see him again.

Standback walks out of the batting cage, and I follow him to the dugout.

I don't like the boy, but I understand him. I run across ten of him for every one who's blessed with a touch of genuine humility. For a ballplayer, a healthy dose of self-assurance is functional. Standback, of course, is off the charts. Fake humility isn't even in his repertoire.

He sits down by himself. It's suitably private. I shouldn't go to this trouble, but it's the right thing to do.

"Mind if I join you?" I ask.

"You're a scout," Standback replies. Not a question. I bet he doesn't know my name, but he remembers me from the mob, from which I mostly observed him.

"Clyde," I say, sitting with a little space between us on the bench. "Clyde Kinlaw."

"Who are you with?"

"I'm not with anyone now," I tell him. "I took a leave of absence. When I get done with a little project I'm working on, I'll go back to scouting for the Loggers."

"They gonna take me?" he asks.

"I don't know," I say. "I turned in my reports. I expect they're seriously considering it."

"That's what my agent thinks."

"A friend of mine with the club asked me to take a closer look," I say. "I've been sort of looking into you, off the field, trying to figure out what makes you tick."

"I don't think that's nobody's business but mine," Standback says, getting riled.

"Five million dollars make it theirs," I say.

"Try ten."

"Ten then. Settle down, Ryne. My intention is to help you here."

He stares at me. "Go on."

"I'm not judgmental, but two people in Haldeman told me you smoke pot quite a bit," I say.

He interrupts me. Quietly, though. It isn't *that* private.

"Oh, bullshit. Who told you that?"

"People with some inside knowledge. People who are right powerful. People who mean you harm," I say. "I didn't just take their word for it. I watched you a little, hanging out with your friends. It was my job. I think they're right, but, as far as I'm concerned, I don't necessarily hold it against you."

"You've seen me smoking weed?"

"Nope. Don't want to. I never did when I was your age, but once I got to the bigs, I did every now and then. Lots of guys did. It helped me manage the pain when my knees went bad. Don't get all pissed off."

He goes silent. He looks at me and takes it in. He's trying to decide if he can trust me. He can. I feel a little guilty that he can.

"I'm not gonna sign with any team that won't put me on the forty-man roster."

He knows that he won't be tested if he's on the forty-man roster. It's one of those labor-contract stipulations between the players' association and management.

"Nobody will do that," I say.

"Somebody will. I know it for a fact."

This kid has an estimation of himself even higher than I thought possible. I have a hard time keeping a straight face.

"You better be ready if whatever that club tells you is a lie."

"I'll just go to Carolina," he says. "I got that option."

"You've got that bluff," I reply. "You go there, you'll have to be even more careful, but that's one area where you're right. It *is* none of my business. What I'm trying to tell you doesn't have a thing to do with baseball. Watch your ass. Be careful. I know for a fact that somebody's trying to set you up. Arrested. The cops are liable to plant a bag of weed on you. Just like they do black kids they're trying to get out of the way. The draft is in the next two weeks. I'd bet it's going to happen soon."

"How in hell can you possibly know this? How do I know you're not just trying to scare me, make me take a lower offer from Portland?"

"That doesn't make a lick of sense," I said, "but I don't really care. I'm telling you this for your own good. Not because I'm your friend. Not because I've got a stake in it, other than knowing a little bit about what pro ball is like. I just feel like I need to give you a fair warning. That's all. Don't go anywhere by yourself. Don't go anywhere high. Don't go anywhere with any on you. Make sure you've got a witness or two."

Not much in the game is worth seeing. I'm satisfied I rattled Standback. Twice he takes called third strikes, and he goes one-for-five with a double. The North team gets clobbered. The head coach's son is a catcher. That means Taiquon doesn't get much of a chance. That catcher couldn't throw out me. I sit across the field, behind the South dugout so I can see inside the North dugout on the first-base side. Taiquon goes into his humble funk. Torin Ferguson sees me and walks around the concourse to sit down next to me.

"This is probably good for you," he says.

"What? Taiquon not playing? It doesn't matter. I feel bad for him. I haven't recognized anybody I know. There might be a couple of sportswriters. They could rave about him in stories, but that doesn't carry no real weight with the pros."

Damned if the coach doesn't put Taiquon in to pitch.

The chubby little catcher who can't throw can't catch Taiquon, either. A burly lefty bat from a Catholic school in Charleston doubles to the right-center field gap off what I expect Taiquon considered a change-up. I expect Taiquon to let loose with one of the cutters I suggested, and it grazes off the catcher's mitt. The runner moves up to third base. Neither Torin nor I say a word.

Taiquon is out of his funk, and he's got a little sweat flowing. He strikes out the batter on three fastballs the catcher manages to snag to end the inning. The South wins, 11-3.

"You want to go eat?" I ask Torin. "I'm guessing you're taking Taiquon home."

"I can't," he says. "His grandma rode down with me."

"Ophelia's here?"

He points to the concourse. She's folding her chair, not one of those canvas jobs everybody sits in nowadays. She's got one of those flimsy ones with strips of striped fabric stretched across to make a seat and back. I can see the rust on the frame from here. I wouldn't sit my fat ass in one.

"That's a good-looking woman for her age," I say.

Torin looks at me kind of crossways and smiles.

"What am I supposed to say? For a black woman. I guess that's what you think a white man's supposed to say."

"I already knew you weren't no racist," Torin says. He chuckles a little, without making a sound.

I laugh, too. We exchange knowing glances that mask what we don't know.

It could be I'm too long without a woman's love. I feel attracted to everyone who crosses my path. Ophelia Sanders. Helen Bauer, the Vosbrinck principal. Drema McLeod.

Drema McLeod would be a possibility, but she'd be like the G.I. Bill. It wouldn't be worth what I'd have to kill to get it. It seems like that's in a song somewhere.

CHAPTER 12

Get Ready to Roll

*M*aybe I've still got some influence in Portland. The Loggers may not know it because Frank Staley Jr. is my conduit. Frank has influence with the club. I've got influence with Frank. He calls me on Monday morning to say the club isn't going to draft Ryne Standback with the third pick in the draft. It's still a little over a week away, but the club is considering a lefthanded pitcher from Roseburg, Oregon, a town in the southern part of the state. I've never heard of the kid, but I haven't been in the state more than a handful of times since the Loggers canned me as manager.

Standback doesn't matter. I've done what I deemed fair. I gave him a fair warning. If I know him, it won't do a bit of good, but I can sleep at night. If he destructs, it will be by himself.

The news I want is about Taiquon Wattson, and Frank has it. He's found Taiquon a team in Texas, north of Dallas, in a city called Buckhead. It's semi-pro, which means Taiquon doesn't get a check, but he does get lodging and meals when he's with the team. I get a modest paycheck, and Taiquon and I are going to live in a little cottage on the shores of something called Lake Texoma, which I'm guessing means the lake is on the border with Oklahoma. I'm going to be the batting instructor and first-base coach of the Buckhead Bucks.

We've got a week to get there and another week to practice before we play. The owner of the team is a businessman named Dreighton Parker. I ask Frank Jr. what kind of business he's in. Frank says he definitely runs a car dealership and is into a lot

85

of other things. He has a music-management company, a small record label, and ...

"A baseball team," I say.

"One of our scouts says he has plenty of money," Frank Jr. says.

"My guess is he ain't making any on this ball team."

"I talked to the guy on the phone. Apparently, he employs a good many of the players in his businesses. The minimum age is eighteen, but I expect a good many of the players are well into their twenties. It'll be good for the Wattson kid to have you to look out for him."

"I ain't gonna be his daddy," I say. "I won't tell him what to do, other than on the ballfield, but I'll tell him what I think when he asks. That's part of the point, Frank. He's as naive as can be. As I've been saying all along, the minors would chew him up and spit him out. He needs to be mentored. That's why I'm willing to do it, that plus I haven't got a whole hell of a lot else to do."

"Call Dreighton Parker as soon as you can," Frank Jr. says. "He's a baseball fan and knows all about you. He's excited to have you on board. The manager – I'm guessing they probably call him a head coach at that level – is an assistant at the local college. Fairly gung-ho fellow, according to Parker."

"I'm just thinking out loud, but I think I'm gonna make a few arrangements, pick up Taiquon, and me and he'll start gradually heading that way. I need this trip to get to know him better, and I can show him some sights along the way. I doubt he's ever been farther away than Atlanta or Columbia in his whole life."

"Well, good luck," Frank says. "Keep in touch. I've got lots of meetings to go to between now and the draft. We invested a little money in the club for you and the boy. They ought to be excited to have you for more reasons than the obvious."

"I appreciate it, Frank."

"I know you do, Clyde. Make this boy into a player for us."

As soon as I get off the phone, I call Ophelia Sanders and ask her how soon she can get her grandson ready to travel.

"A day," she says. "He's excited. High school graduation was last night."

"Take two," I reply. "I'll be down to pick him up early Monday morning. I'm taking him to play ball in Texas."

"Texas? Good God Almighty."

"I'll look out for him, Ophelia. We're gonna share a little cabin on a lake that's probably a good bit like Thurmond."

"How long y'all gon' be out there, Mr. Kinlaw?"

"Lord, Ophelia, for God's sake, call me Clyde," I say. "Season's six weeks long. There may be some playoffs or whatnot. If everything goes the way I hope it will, I'll have him in a pro-ball uniform by the end of summer. We may ship him off to Arizona for fall pro ball, but I don't know anything for certain. It just depends on how things work out. Don't worry. I'm not putting all this effort into your baby boy just to have him fail. If I didn't believe in him, I wouldn't do it."

"I'm grateful, Clyde, but I sure am gonna miss him."

"I'll make sure he keeps in touch, ma'am. I'll get him his own phone as quick as I can get around to it," I say. "Taiquon's not there, is he?"

"No, he's working. You need to talk to him?"

"I've got a trip halfway across the country to talk to him," I say.

CHAPTER 13

My Canterbury Tales

I hope this adventure with Taiquon will relieve the ones I have in my dreams. They all involve going somewhere and being unable to get back home. Last night it was some sort of festival. When it ended, I found myself alone without any means of transportation, so I resolved to walk. It's always a ridiculous distance – thirty or forty miles, at least – and I encounter all sorts of obstacles along the way. This one involves a band of friendly hippies in the parking lot of a shopping center, late at night after all the stores have closed. They aren't threatening. They neither befriend nor sneer at me. I don't inform them of my plight. I couldn't seem to escape them, though, to continue on my walk home through the darkness.

The only two people with whom I've ever shared the dreams are Dub Whatley, my old coach, and Jimmy Daggett, my lawyer. They're my two best friends, I reckon. Frank Staley Jr. and I are friends, but it doesn't really count if communication is ninety-nine percent over the phone. Text messages don't count at all. At best, texting is between friendly acquaintances. My definition of a friend is narrow. I don't have more than five I count. At the height of my career, they never numbered more than ten. Hundreds consider me a friend. I give Lawyer Daggett a hard time because his profession is composed of the biggest name-droppers on earth. If a lawyer shakes another man's hand, he tells everyone they are close friends. Jimmy is better than most. That has something to do with why he's my lawyer. He was my agent when I needed one. I hope I'm going to need him soon, but this time his work will be related to getting a square deal for Taiquon Wattson.

Dub is a living, breathing defier of stereotypes. He's a coach with the wisdom of a poet. Before he retired, Dub taught shop, or whatever it is they call it nowadays. As I recall, shop teachers were responsible for getting their students to build paddles for coaches to punish athletes thirty-five years ago. I think one of Dub's classes was called "mechanical drawing." I reckon they drew a paddle up before they carved it out of wood. I never took shop. Before the Portland Loggers came knocking, I was strictly college prep. It was Dub, though, who got me to read books that hadn't been assigned for English classes. He introduced me to Larry McMurtry, Elmore Leonard, Dick Francis, Kurt Vonnegut, and John Irving. It sure made lots of minor-league bus trips bearable. When I told Dub about my dreams, he compared them to *The Canterbury Tales*. I read enough of them to see his point, but the English of Geoffrey Chaucer's time is hard to endure, what with all the old-fashioned spellings that are now only seen in the names of streets in pretentious subdivisions. *Ye Olde Boulevarde*. Lawyer Daggett and his wife, Peatsy, live on a street by that name. The *boulevarde* to my house is paved in gravel, and it's needed a few more loads for about ten years now. Jimmy's helped me with my culture, too. He and Dub got me started playing golf. Ted Williams said the hardest thing in sports was hitting a baseball. If Ted said it, it's true, but hitting a golf ball is harder for me. I even played tennis with Jimmy till my knees went bad. He still plays it at the age of seventy. Jimmy will live to be a hundred. I'll be lucky if I ever collect a penny of social security. My lawyer thinks life's too short. For the past five years, I've thought about it for too long.

That's one more reason Taiquon Wattson is important to me. Building him up might just do the same for me.

As usual, it's more likely for me to catch Jimmy Daggett at Crosley's Office Supplies than in his office. I had a hunch I'd find him and Dub sitting around in swivel chairs. One time Vern sold Lawyer Daggett's favorite chair, and Jimmy told him to order another, and he'd pay for it, just to sit in when he and Dub were holding court. Now it's got stenciled red letters on the back: *Not for Sale.* I bring a sack of Hardee's sausage biscuits with me, knowing Vern will supply the coffee. It doesn't surprise me that Dub and Jimmy have a tee time at eleven. It doesn't surprise me when they ask me to join them. I say I'd love to, but I'm heading to Texas.

"How long are you gon' be gone?" Dub asks.

"Couple months."

"You're really going through with it."

"Yep. Long shot, but what the hell."

"That's what you wanted to talk to me about, huh?" Jimmy asks. "Beverly said you stopped by."

"It wasn't that important," I say. "I just wanted to lay some groundwork. If everything works out with this kid, I'm gonna need you to write up a low-grade, free-agent contract. I'm not gonna trust some standardized piece of paper from the ballclub. I didn't when I played for 'em, neither."

"How well I remember," Jimmy says. "I'll be here if you need my services. I reckon you can still afford my services."

"I expect you know the answer to that better than I do," I say.

"Who's gonna watch your house?" Vern asks.

"Ryan's home from college." Ryan is my sister Elaine's son. "I think he's fairly delighted to get out of their house."

"You want me to check on him every now and then?" Dub asks.

"Don't do nothing to make him think you're my spy," I say. "Just pull 'bout halfway down the road every so often. As long as there ain't a band of Rastafarians playing reggae on the back deck, leave 'em be."

"Ah, Ryan's a good boy," Jimmy says. "I'm satisfied he'll use a rubber."

"It ain't like he ain't been in college two years already," I say. "Ryan might be the last kid on earth who still thinks I'm cool.

I'm a certified loser in the art of being a parent. Being an uncle's easy. It's like checking a kid out of the library."

"When you striking out?" Dub asks.

"I've been striking out figuratively ever since I stopped striking out literally. I'm hoping Taiquon Wattson is a fastball right down the middle. One I can drive. I'm driving down to Vosbrinck to pick him soon as I get done wasting time with y'all boys. I'm in no hurry. We got a week to get to Buckhead, Texas. We're gonna take our time. I still don't know Taiquon a tenth as much as I'm gonna."

"Let us know how it's going if you think of it," Vern says.

"I'll keep my contracting iron warm," Jimmy says.

CHAPTER 14
A Misplaced Metaphor

All I know about Taiquon Wattson is insignificant compared to what I am about to learn. He's quiet. I'm going to draw him out. He's different on the field. He's bold, confident, competitive, and tough. Away from the game – any game, apparently – Taiquon is unsure of himself. The playing field is where he demonstrates his worth. The classroom is where he doesn't even try. He has few social skills. He doesn't know how to drive a car. In a small stroke of genius, it occurred to me to put Taiquon's bicycle under the rollback cover of my truck. Taiquon is silent. I am thinking to myself that I hope Buckhead, Texas, has a decent black population. I'd hate for Taiquon to get hassled for riding a bicycle through a white neighborhood. He's probably pondering what his new world is going to be like. If I were him, I wouldn't be talking right now, and I talk a lot. Always have.

It's a good thing I didn't drive west across the river. I just wanted to get on I-20 because we're going to ride it for a long time. We're not going to ride it far today, though.

"When's the last time you been to a ballgame?" I ask.

"Sir?"

"Not to play in. To watch. When's the last time you watched a baseball game."

He thought. "I don't remember none."

"Well, Taiquon, that is about to change," I say. "There's a minor league team in Augusta. I'm not sure they're at home, but if not, we'll just keep on driving. There's minor-league baseball all over the place in the South."

We're in luck. The Augusta Greenjackets are playing the Columbia Fireflies. I find my way to the stadium by following the directions offered by a billboard. If I hadn't seen it, I would have resorted to my phone. The good news is they're at home. The bad news is that we're way too early. I don't know a lot about Augusta, Georgia. I might have played there in the minors, but, if so, it was a different stadium. The minors have changed a lot. I bet there's not a single park still operating that I played in. The old fairgrounds park in Toledo. Rickwood Field in Birmingham. The old Louisville Redbirds played in a park weird for both sports played in it, baseball and University of Louisville football. Most parks nowadays have been built within the past twenty-five years. Birmingham has replaced old Rickwood twice.

The Greenjackets play in a brand-new palace. A high-rise apartment building sits behind the left-field wall. I wonder if all the apartments overlook the field. If not, I wonder how much less the ones that don't cost. Upon further review, I discover the building is a hotel. It's not finished yet, and this is a development in which the ballpark is the centerpiece and the first edifice completed.

If I'm not mistaken, the park is in South Carolina. It's near the Savannah River, but if I'm not having a senior moment, it's in what is known as North Augusta, South Carolina.

I don't ask Taiquon what he wants to eat. We're going to have plenty of opportunities to succumb to junk food, and I certainly don't want to fatten Taiquon – or me, either, for that matter – on the way west. I instinctively tilt the wheel toward where there's bound to be shopping areas and find a Golden Corral. Neither of us has eaten since early this morning, but a buffet comes in handy because I fill up on as much meat and vegetables as I want and back off on the bread and sweets. Taiquon, who has no discernible fat on that part of his anatomy that I have witnessed, shows me that it's not for lack of appetite. I stick with baked chicken, green beans, broccoli, and spinach. Taiquon eats some of that and everything else.

After we eat too much – Taiquon has the enthusiasm for a buffet a younger child might have for a playhouse – I realize that Augusta National means nothing to him. He's never heard of the Masters. When I tell him it's a golf tournament, he says, "Oh, yeah. I heard something 'bout that." I took him back to the ballpark, where we were still an hour early.

I have a pass that gets me and "a guest" into any game in the country, though I haven't used it in a while because the Loggers don't ever send me to evaluate minor leaguers anymore. I don't particularly want to mingle with any other scouts, so I ask the fellow in the ticket window not to put us behind the plate. He gives us a pair of tickets down the third-base line. I doubt I'm going to bump into any suspicious peers. Most scouts are notoriously late arrivals. I see one guy I recognize leaning on the cage during batting practice. He's a roving batting instructor for the Giants, the Augusta parent club, but he's not scanning the crowd.

Taiquon and I take our seats.

"I'm really looking forward to this," I say. "I can't remember the last time I went to a ballgame just to watch it. Baseball is the only game that's relaxing to watch, Taiquon. It's not relaxing when you're watching the Red Sox play the Yankees, but a minor-league game is the best place in the world for people to talk."

I imagine Taiquon thinking, *oh, boy, here we go*, but he doesn't roll his eyes. He's just taking it in, and it's my impression that he likes what he sees. The park in Lexington, South Carolina, where he played in the North-South Game, is the best place he's ever played. This yard makes that look like a sandlot. It's average to left, short to right, and a bit shallow to center.

It's hard for me to pay attention to a game when I'm in the stands unless I'm either listening via earbuds to the local radio broadcast or keeping score and taking notes. My mind tends to wander to little things, whether it's the interaction between kids five rows below, the style of a hot dog vendor, or some nuance in a batter's stance or a pitcher's delivery. My mind flits around as if it were a hummingbird in a flower garden. Taiquon, as usual, has little to say other than "yes, sir," but he's enjoying himself, taking in the atmosphere like a kid at a circus. No one is more entertained by an oafish mascot or amused by "lucky" fans who get to circle themselves dizzy shuffling around an upright bat, then wobble and fall as they attempt to win a race.

"You ever been drunk, Taiquon?" I ask.

"No, sir."

"If you were, you wouldn't have to circle a baseball bat to have a race like that."

I recognize a kid playing for Columbia. He's an outfielder I scouted. As I recall, he seriously considered going to college. He had scholarship offers from good schools: Duke, Vanderbilt, and Virginia, and I think the last was where he had been headed. He was from Chester, I think. Stautner. Trey Stautner. It was three years ago. The Mets drafted him in the first round. That means it's his third year of pro ball. A first-rounder ought to be higher than Low A by now. I can't blame him for signing. He probably got somewhere north of two million. I look at the scoreboard. He's batting .206. I'm partial to minor-league instruction, but this kid probably should have gone to Virginia.

Stautner's swing is too big. He can't lay off a slider, away, in the dirt. Stautner takes a rip at everything. I guarantee he strikes out about twice as much as is acceptable. New York's got too much invested in him to cast him aside ... yet. The best thing that could happen to him is to get traded. Maybe another organization could straighten him out. If the Mets could, they would have by now.

Taiquon doesn't have much to say. He's still taking it all in.

In the third inning, he says, "Man, they throw hard down here."

"You'll be fine," I reply. "You just need some experience against this kind of pitching. You're gonna get it if we have to go all the way to Texas."

"You sure got a lot of confidence in me." Taiquon says it *con-fuh-DENCE*.

Columbia is batting in the fourth when he asks, "How far is Texas?"

"Well, where we going is about a thousand miles," I say. "So far, we've gone about thirty."

"Yes, sir."

"If I just took off for Texas, and drove it straight through, I could make it in a day and half a night, but we're gonna take our time. Between here and there, we're just gonna stop and see whatever strikes our fancy. Maybe a few more ball games. Do you see a sign about something you think's worth seeing? I'll pull it off. We got a week. We need a week. We still got some gettin' to know each left to do."

"Yes, sir."

I worry about Taiquon getting lonesome. He's bound to miss home. It's all he knows. If I put him on a train, gave him some money, and tried to tell him how to get there, he might not make it. Even if he did, he might run away. I remember the story my dad used to tell about the kid who worked with us on the farm and signed a scholarship to play football at The Citadel. Dad agreed to give him a ride down to Charleston, where he was due to enroll and report for practice. The Citadel is a military school that was then a bit more known for hazing than it is now. Jerry Fowler didn't make it. Dad used to say Jerry got back to Youngville before he did.

I wonder what happened to Jerry Fowler. I haven't thought of him in twenty years.

It occurs to me that this is something my dad might've done. I'm going to do it right, though. I'm not just dropping Taiquon off. I'm gonna stay out there with him and make sure he keeps his head on straight. We both need this trip. We've got to get to know each other a lot better. I need to learn how to read him. I doubt he's ever going to get talkative.

The Fireflies pull ahead with four runs in the seventh, and I ask Taiquon if he's ready to go. He wouldn't tell me if he wasn't.

"Yes, sir."

We hit Interstate Twenty and barrel through the night in the direction of Atlanta. Taiquon dozes off. I stop before we get there and get myself a mug of coffee. Then I awaken him when we get into town so that he can ogle at the skyscrapers. I take a little detour so that I can show him Turner Field.

"This is where the Braves used to play," I tell him when we stop in a parking lot."

"Used to?"

"They built a new ballpark out on the northwest side, probably ten, fifteen miles from here, at least."

"What for?" Taiquon asks. "This looks pretty nice."

"It is," I say. "There really wasn't any excuse for it. The people who run the team decided there were more folks out there with enough money to buy tickets."

"White folks," he says.

"Yep. That's pretty much it."

Taiquon is talking about more than a ballpark when he says, "I ain't got no use for no Atlanta."

We get back in the pickup and continue west until we get to Carrollton, a college town with motels on the exits, and get a room at an Econolodge a few blocks south of the interstate. It's late, going on two in the morning. I sleep well. Taiquon says he did, too.

"Yes, sir."

What seems like a relatively clean dump to me seems fit for a king to Taiquon. I go with him to the free breakfast and find that one thing he knows how to do is drink coffee. I'll have to get him a discount mug at the next truck stop. I have some raisin bran. Taiquon likes Rice Krispies. I like the cheese danish. He prefers the cherry.

About an hour down the road, I see a recreation park on the side of the highway and ask Taiquon if he'd like to stretch his legs.

"Yes, sir."

I start thinking about ways to get him to say "no, sir," and consider asking if he'd like to break his neck.

This is Oxford, Alabama. I park the truck next to a soccer field between two parks, one meant for baseball and the other for softball. I get out and literally stretch my legs. Arthritis in both knees makes me stiff as a board whenever I sit still. It took me halfway up the steps to escape a limp when we left the ballgame in Augusta. Taiquon stretches his legs a little more dramatically. He's like a greyhound let loose from a starting gate. He takes off running at a pace that strikes me as torrid and goes around the edge of the chain-link fences of all three fields. It was probably about a half mile. When he gets back and catches his breath, I ask him if he wants to screw a donkey.

"Sir?"

I lie and say it's just another way to say "play catch."

"Yes, sir."

I didn't get a "no, sir," just a "sir?" It's progress.

We play catch for about twenty minutes. I need to get back in spring training shape before we get to Texas. After we get back on the road, it's only a few miles to Talladega Superspeedway, the gigantic NASCAR track where I've seen a couple of races. A friendly security guard lets us walk inside and sit in the grandstands near the fourth turn for a while. I can tell from the size of Taiquon's eyes that the track, somewhere between two and three miles around, might as well be the Pyramids of Egypt to his mind.

My lack of planning, and lack of care about planning, becomes evident when I realize that, while the Birmingham Barons have a home game scheduled since it's a Sunday, the game is in the afternoon and about over by the time I pull the truck down the street of the new palace in downtown. Instead, we eat at a barbecue joint a few blocks away, beat the postgame crowd and head back down the interstate to Tuscaloosa, where I show Taiquon where Alabama plays football. He knows all about Alabama, and it occurs to me that what he had cared most about before I came along was college football. I wish I'd seen him play.

I look at my road map and decide to head northwest through Mississippi to Memphis. We get a room just shy of the border, and I think about taking Taiquon to Graceland, but I figure he might know more about Martin Luther King than Elvis, so I take him instead to Beale Street and the Lorraine Motel, where the civil rights leader was assassinated. We listen to some blues and eat more barbecue, this time the dry-rubbed Memphis kind, then we catch the Memphis Redbirds against the Oklahoma City Dodgers in a stadium even more lavish than the one in Birmingham. The Redbirds are the Triple-A club of the Cardinals, Birmingham is Double-A, White Sox, and AutoZone is almost a scaled-down big-league park. Tall buildings rise above left field in a way that reminds me a little of Cleveland for some reason.

I'm happy to see Taiquon strike up a ballpark friendship with a kid sitting next to him who's roughly his age. I don't want to interfere, so I go find a scorecard and start following the game. I'm mildly aware that Taiquon is telling the other kid about how he's headed to Texas to play semi-pro baseball himself, and the white man sitting next to him is his coach, which is the first time to my knowledge he's referred to me that way. The other kid's a city boy, much more sophisticated in the ways of the world, and he becomes fascinated with Taiquon's story.

I'm amazed at how talkative Taiquon can be when he's talking to another kid his age. He talks about watching a game in

Augusta, Georgia, and then seeing the big race track in Alabama, and the big stadium where the Crimson Tide plays, and how he understands now exactly what happened when Dr. King got shot, and the kid, whose name is some variation of Rashad or Rasheed, most likely with an apostrophe somewhere, asks him if it was tough being cooped up in a car all that way. Taiquon tells him it's a truck, not a car, and it's plenty comfortable.

Then he says to Rashad, "Yesterday we stopped in some place called Oxford, Alabama, and screwed a donkey."

After I managed to stop coughing, I ask Taiquon if he minds going to get me a Diet Coke, hand him some money, and tell him to get anything he wants.

Lest Rashad likens me to a character in *Deliverance*, or alerts the authorities via his cell phone, I explain how I had said that to Taiquon while trying to get him to say something other than "yes, sir" to everything I asked.

"I told him 'screw a donkey' was another way of saying 'play catch.'"

I'm satisfied Rashad is going to tell that story far and wide. After a nice, long moratorium, it's entirely possible I will.

CHAPTER 15

A Hole in the Swing

*a*fter a night at a Days Inn located in eastern Arkansas, Taiquon and I stop south of Little Rock and eat at a very large and just as mediocre buffet just off the interstate, and by now, I'm holding back a little because we're getting to Texas a bit early for my taste. Of all things, I decided to stop off at a diamond mine. Yes, a diamond mine, or a former one that is now a state park. It kills considerable time, mainly because what I had envisioned as conveniently near the four-lane ends up requiring a considerable ride that just happens to take us through Delight, Arkansas, which memory tells me is the hometown of one Glen Campbell. You'd never know it.

There's a crater of diamonds, one where a volcano brought the gems to the surface, oh, 95 million years ago, a fact that blows Taiquon's mind when he reads it on a plaque. There's a swimming pool there at the crater, and I encourage Taiquon to take a dip. The denim shorts he's wearing are as close to trunks as anything he's packed, and he splashes around and dives repeatedly to the bottom while I sit on a bench checking out the latest news on my trusty Samsung.

The president is off in some foreign country showing his ass to our allies. The Loggers are eleven games under .500 already. Minnesota is about twice as good as anyone expected, and Seattle, which got off to a fast start, has all but disappeared. The world-champion Red Sox are mired in third place. In the National League, the Dodgers and Braves are pulling away in their respective divisions. It occurs to me that I promised Ophelia I would get Taiquon a phone of his own, and I make a note on my phone to do so when we get to Texas. We cross into Texas at Texarkana – the old song "Cotton Fields" comes to mind, "down in Louisiana, just about a mile from Texarkana," which is impossible because Louisiana is about a half hour's drive – and spend the night in Paris, Texas, which leaves us with a Saturday to kill. We're supposed to be at some sort of social occasion in Buckhead on Sunday. Taiquon and I get up early, and I continue on as a tour guide as we visit the Don Meredith Museum in the Mount Vernon fire department and the Sam Rayburn Museum in Bonham and spend a few minutes. I figure that between Dandy Don, the late Dallas Cowboys quarterback and television analyst, and the longtime Speaker of the House of Representatives, Taiquon is getting a decent baseline on the culture of Texas.

Taiquon is an earnest young man. Though he has never heard of either Meredith or Rayburn, he is reasonably interested. This would not be the case if I were traveling with a young man versed in the use of a mobile phone, and, as we walk back to the truck from examining the artifacts of a long-dead politician, I start chuckling to myself as I imagine taking a similar trip with Ryne Standback. Little do I know this snippet of thought is portentous. We check into a motel on the outskirts of Buckhead, unpack, and Taiquon and I head south to Frisco, there to attend yet another minor league game.

I did not know that Standback had been drafted by the Houston Astros and assigned to its Double-A affiliate, the Corpus Christi Hooks. The Hooks are playing the Frisco Roughriders, and Taiquon notices Standback's name in the batting order before I do.

So, the Astros sent Standback to the Texas League. It had to be at the insistence of his agent, whom I've not had the pleasure of meeting. The scoreboard lists Standback as batting seventh, playing first base, and hitting .166. The average does not surprise me. I give Taiquon a twenty and ask him to buy a program, two if he wants one, and bring me a Diet Dr. Pepper if he thinks of it.

I lean back and take a few deep breaths. I've never been in a ballpark similar to this one. It's nestled in something of a planned community, overlooked by high-rise apartments or condominiums and shopping outlets. The tickets are priced at minor-league levels, but parking and concessions seem more like the major leagues. Taiquon returns with programs for each of us and my Diet Dr. Pepper.

"You didn't want anything?" I ask. "I mean, to drink."

"No, sir," He says.

"How much did two programs and a drink cost?"

"Seventeen dollars and forty-two cents," he says. "I got your change."

"Hells bells," I say as I grab my wallet again. "Here's another twenty, get yourself something to eat."

At least we didn't have to pay our way in. I take a sip from the drink. I wouldn't mind a beer. For the first time in about five years, I wish I had a pack of cigarettes, not that I could smoke one here. I hate it when the bad guys win.

A stat sheet is stuck inside the program. Standback has four home runs and fifteen runs batted in. He started out reasonably well. At the moment, he has two hits in his last twenty-nine at-bats.

"What do you think about Ryne Standback?" I ask Taiquon.

"I hope he does good," he says. "You know, he and I have played against each other."

"This game is going to be a good lesson, Taiquon. When you play at this level, guys like me pay close attention. When they spot a weakness, word gets around. All you start getting are pitches you can't hit. You gotta make adjustments, and cure your weaknesses. Know what I mean?"

"Yes, sir."

"All I know about Standback is what I saw scouting him. You know I noticed you when the Loggers sent me to scout Standback, right?"

"Coach Ferguson told me that," he says.

"Standback stands off the plate. He's trying to extend his arms," I say. "Middle of the plate in, belt high and a little below, and he's gonna clean it out, but he can't cover the plate. The way to pitch him is high and tight, off the plate. Good chance he'll swing. You're setting up for a breaking ball, preferably a slider or a cutter, low and outside. He's got that swing they're teaching everybody. Open stance then strides straight into the pitch. That far from the plate, he can't cover it even if it stays up in the zone. He's got to lunge at it, and he won't take it to the opposite field. Have you ever seen him hit it the other way? I haven't."

"No, sir," Taiquon says after thinking for a few seconds. In spite of all those "yes, sirs" and "no, sirs," I like the fact that Taiquon thinks about it first. He may not tell me much, but he's not just saying what I want to hear.

Standback makes me look like a prophet. He bats with two out in the second inning and strikes out on a slider off the plate and in the dirt. In the bottom of the third, a lefthanded batter hits an average grounder two steps to his right. He barely takes one. The second baseman gets to it in the outfield grass, but the pitcher is late covering first, and Standback doesn't even try to get back. It sets off a four-run inning for the Rough Riders, who have little caricatures of Teddy Roosevelt on the fronts of their caps. Standback ought to be in Florida Instructional League, Rookie ball at the highest. He's in way over his head here, and his ego blocks his mind from thinking.

Going to this game is a great accident. Taiquon has none of Standback's obvious weaknesses. Taiquon is going to have to prove he can keep up with ninety-mile-an-hour heat. I doubt he's ever hit against it.

In the eighth inning, with the Hooks trailing by six runs, Standback hits a hanging curve ball out of the park. He goes one-for-four with three strikeouts.

"A mistake," I tell Taiquon. "All he hits are mistakes."

"But he sure can hit a mistake a long way," Taiquon says.

"That he can, my boy. That he can."

CHAPTER 16
The Outside World

⚜

I finally get around to buying Taiquon a cell phone, which I add to my account. In fact, I upgrade mine, which I can figure out while I'm teaching Taiquon how to use his. There's no time for that now, so I tell him to read the manual when he gets a chance, and when he gets done, I'll put a few numbers in it for him – most definitely, his grandmother's, who is probably worried sick – and show him what it'll do.

An office that reminds me of where the ranger lives at a state park is where I pick up keys for our new abode at 104-A Parker Ranch Road. It's rustic for a duplex, similar to the cabins on a nearby lake where my friends once partied back in the day. There's time to move in thoroughly but not much else. Everyone is getting together at five at the home of the Bucks' owner, and all I know about him is his name, Dreighton Parker, but the place is nearby, and I've got a hunch that Parker owns our cabin and where we are headed is Parker Ranch. It's cheaper that way.

My advice to Taiquon is that he write down his new phone number, and that way if any of his teammates want to swamp him with theirs, he can tell them to text him.

"What's a text?" he asks.

My God.

There's time for Taiquon to call Ophelia. I tell him to go out on the back porch and talk to her privately. I punch in his grandmother's number, and when it starts ringing, I tell him to go on outside and talk with her if she answers. I hear him say "hello" as he closes the door behind him.

I turn down the thermostat from eighty to seventy and sit down in a chair. I haven't unpacked the laptop, so I text Jimmy Daggett to tell him I've added Taiquon to my cellular account. My lawyer is paying my bills while I'm away. I reckon he pays most of them electronically. I gave him all my passwords and the like. It's good to have a friend I can trust. Jimmy keeps plenty of money in my checking account. My bank has more locations in north Texas than it does in South Carolina. Jimmy discovered that. He anticipates my every move. It doesn't hurt to have an agent who once sat in front of me in French class. Whatever he charges me is worth it.

Taiquon spends about a half hour on the screened-in porch. He returns and says his grandma wants to talk to me.

"My boy sounds like you treatin' him right," she says.

"I'm glad to hear he feels that way. We had a right good time. Look, Ophelia, we've got to go over to this cookout or something and meet the team. I promise you that I'll call you first thing in the morning," I tell her, and she says that'll be fine.

I call up a map of Lake Texoma on my phone. It looks like a skinny dragon with a long tail. I tell Taiquon that's Oklahoma on the other side, just like Georgia is on the other side where he lives.

Dreighton Parker is about what I expected. He's wearing docksiders and a pair of khaki cargo pants, a short-sleeved plaid shirt with pearl snaps for buttons, and a bolo tie. He cries out for cowboy boots, but it's hot, it's the lake, and he's got a Bucks blue cap on instead of a Stetson.

Texans and South Carolinians both talk Southern, but the Texans enunciate better. Back where Taiquon and I came from, we drawl. A good word of comparison is "Charlie," which Texans like Parker pronounce like it's spelled. I say it "Cholly." Charlie Gabbard is the team's manager, or, at this level, head coach. I introduce Taiquon to them, then I tell him to go meet his new teammates. Tables full of barbecue are lined up out in the wooded area leading down to the banks of the lake. Tubs full of iced-down beer are at the ends of each table. I can't tell, but I reckon there are some cans of Coca-Cola and the like mixed in.

Parker, Gabbard, and I sit on the back deck of his mansion. Parker sends a pert young woman to bring us some beer, and I could use one. She returns with a bucket full of Lone Star.

"So, Taiquon's just eighteen years old, I hear," Gabbard says.

"Yep," I reply, "but he's young for his age. He didn't have a cell phone till I bought him one this morning."

"Hell, he is from Petticoat Junction," Parker says. "All the other players are at least twenty-one. If he slips up and drinks a beer, ain't nobody gonna say nothing."

"That would be quite a surprise," I say.

"I see he's enjoying the fruit punch," Parker says.

"I don't reckon it's spiked," I say.

"I wouldn't be surprised," Parker replies.

Oh, well. *Que sera, sera.*

The three of us finish our first beer – well, my first beer – and mosey on down to the tables to fill up a plate of brisket, German sausage, and corn on the cob. I take a sip of the "punch" and discover it's what is called "sangria wine" out here. We get down to some serious eating and talk mainly about my career. I'm taking it as it comes. If Taiquon gets drunk for the first time, well, it was coming sooner or later, anyway. As my long, gone daddy used to say, "Chaps love to play."

Parker tells me he's got five car lots, and he's happy to give Taiquon the use of an old trade-in from the lot. I tell him Taiquon doesn't have a driver's license.

"The team doesn't practice till five in the evening, does it, Charlie?" Parker asks.

"That's right," Gabbard replies.

"There'll be plenty of time to take care of things like that," Parker says.

"How's he gonna get a Texas driver's license?" I ask.

"Car dealers got a heap of contacts at the highway department," Parker says. "Just make sure he doesn't flunk the test."

"The season ain't but six weeks," I say. "We brought his bicycle with us."

"Well, the offer's there," Parker says.

"I appreciate it, Mr. Parker."

"Cut out that Mr. Parker shit. Just call me Dray. You were a big-league ballplayer. I expect we're 'bout the same age. And this here's Charlie. The ballplayers call him that, too."

"Ah'ight," I say. "Dray it is."

Charlie says the two other assistant coaches are out there with the players. One's the pitching coach. The other coaches third and runs the bullpen after the first few innings, at which point Charlie takes over. He says I'll be in charge of hitting and coaching first, but he says things won't be too specialized, and he'd appreciate my help with the infield. The coaches are available to hit in a pinch, and one is handy for mop-up duty out of the pen. A good many play in college, and that's why, technically, they make their spending money working for Dray.

"I reckon Taiquon's free and clear, having finished school," Dray says. "I'll pay him just like I do you, but if he'd like to make some money on the side, it's there for him once he gets his driver's license."

"I'll think about it," I say. "Between that bicycle and my truck, I reckon I can get him where he needs to be. Let's start him out slow."

When the night falls, a country band shows up, and lights come on to illuminate the woods. I follow Charlie down there, and he introduces me to the other coaches, but I can't half get their names because the music is playing so loud. I know of three states – Tennessee, Kentucky, and Texas – where it seems like everybody can play the guitar. I can play a little, and if I drink three more beers, I might just sit down and borrow one.

The band, Andy Driftwood, and His Drifters, takes a break, and I walk down to the dock, where Taiquon is engaged in a conversation over whether or not he can swim across the lake and back. This is not a good sign.

"Having a good time?" I ask, catching Taiquon by surprise.

He tries to straighten up. His new friends start laughing.

"How's that punch, hotshot?"

"It's good," he says. "I like it."

"You know, it's a little stronger than Kool-Aid."

"That's what I just heard," he says.

"If you try to swim that lake, we might just drown," I say, "'cause you can bet I'm coming in after you."

"Yes, sir."

It was comforting to hear him say it. I knew he was going to grow up in a hurry, but I wasn't expecting him to start so soon.

A good-looking Mexican gal had her eyes on him.

I'm not his daddy – he hasn't got one – and I know better than to preach. I just hope he'll talk to me and let me nudge him in the right direction. I reckon things could be worse. I could have Ryne Standback to look after.

CHAPTER 17

Growing Up Is Hard to Do

J get up early, set up the coffeemaker in the kitchen, and stand nearby to see if the K-cup works. If it hasn't been used in a few days, the flow starts only after I bang the top of the machine a few times. As usual, this does the trick. I haven't got time to clean it right now, and it's a long shot whether or not I can remember to buy the distilled vinegar it takes to do so. I walk out on the porch, sit down in one of Dreighton Parker's rocking chairs and start reading my phone. I reply to Frank Staley Jr.'s text and let him know Taiquon Wattson and I are safe and sound and getting ready for our first practice with the Buckhead Bucks. Predictably, Frank Jr. replies that I should keep in touch.

The Loggers won 4-3 in Oakland. Since the last I checked, Portland is three games above .500, though still eight games under overall. In Frisco, Ryne Standback hit another homer but was one-for-four, and the other three at-bats were strikeouts. Somebody didn't get the memo about eschewing the fastballs. I bet it was on a three-ball count.

I'm mindful it's an hour later back east, so I go ahead and ring Ophelia Sanders. She's expecting it. I can tell because she answers before the second ring.

"Hello. Clyde? How's my boy?"

"Oh, he's fine," I say. "He met all his teammates last night. Practice is late this afternoon."

"Seem like they some good boys?"

"They're all older than him," I say. "We're staying on a lake just across from Oklahoma. Lake Texoma. Taiquon loves the water. That's about all that hasn't changed."

"Watch him, Clyde. He ain't never had a chance to travel."

"Believe me, Ophelia, I know. He's gonna grow up out here. The trick is not to let him grow up too fast."

I expect she knows there's more to it than I'm saying. We descend into small talk. I tell her it's just about as hot but a good bit drier than back home. No need to get her worried and shaken up. While I'm half-listening to Ophelia, a young Hispanic – I think John Wayne might have called him a Texican – walks out on another section of the duplex'sscreened-in porch, sees me sitting there, and goes back inside. I hear a window fan switch on in the window. Hmm. Surely, if this side has air conditioning, that side does. I finish my coffee, walk back across the living room, sit it down and go knock on Taiquon's door. On the second try, he tells me to come in.

"How are you feeling, hotshot?"

"I reckon I been better. You?"

"Oh, I'm fine," I say. "I've been drunk before. You?"

"No, sir, not to speak of."

I sit down on the bed. Taiquon looks a little older.

"Well, you want my advice?"

"Yes, sir."

"Good. You got to practice this afternoon. You get up. Answer what your innards are saying, and, by that, I mean to relieve yourself and sit in the toilet if you need to till something comes out, and then you need to get some sweat up. Either take a ride on your bicycle or take a nice jog. Meanwhile, I'll go out and get us something to eat. You get done, and you'll be hungry. Ah'ight?"

"Okay," he says.

"You want some coffee first?"

"I reckon."

"Well, I know you didn't drink till last night. You might as well get used to not doing one without the other," I say.

He's sort of ashamed because he feels like he needs to be. He doesn't look entirely genuine. I got back into the kitchen and pop in another K-cup.

"You'd probably like it better with a little milk in it," I say, "but we ain't got none yet. I drink it black with Sweet 'n' Low. It's hot right now. Let it sit a bit; then take a sip to see if it's cooled down enough to suit your tongue."

I decide shaving is unnecessary but take a quick shower. When I get out, I can see Taiquon pedaling up the road on his bicycle. I put on some cargo shorts and a tee shirt, slip into my sneakers, and see that Taiquon has drunk his coffee. I reckon he learns fast, and that's what I'm afraid of.

At the first intersection, there's a CVS, and I buy the basic groceries one finds there: milk, eggs, smoked sausage, margarine, a twelve-pack of Dr. Pepper for Taiquon and Diet Dr. Pepper for me, bread, mayonnaise, mustard, cheese slices, three boxes of cereal, a few cans of soup, some saltines, and assorted health and beauty aids. I decide I'll wait till tomorrow to fix breakfast and swing by the Whataburger for sausage-and-egg biscuits, and hash brown sticks. Taiquon's back by the time I am.

"Feel better?" I ask.

"Yes, sir. That done the trick."

"Let's have some breakfast." I pass him the bag. "How about a cold glass of milk to wash it down."

Neither of us has much to say for a minute. As expected, Taiquon is hungry. After a couple of minutes, he initiates a conversation, which is unusual for him.

"Mister Parker, he says he'll let me have a car to use," he says. "I didn't tell him I don't have a license."

"I told him. He says he can help you get one, even out here in Texas, 'cause he knows some people in the highway department."

"Cool." This is a word I have never heard Taiquon say.

"I'm kind of surprised you'd be interested in driving," I say.

"I got to learn some time," he says.

"True. I reckon that's one more thing I'll have to teach you."

"Well, I been watching you drive all the way out here. I reckon I can learn."

"Taiquon, I don't suppose you wanting to drive has anything to do with the cute little girl I saw making eyes at you last night?"

A little bashfulness rises up in him. He smiles, sees the look on my face, and says, "A little."

I get up and start putting cereal and soup on the shelves and eggs and the like in the refrigerator. When I return, and Taiquon is finishing the last of the hash browns, I slide a plastic-and-paper container across the table.

"What's her name?" I ask.

"Juana. Her full name is Juanita, but she says everybody calls her Juana. Her older brother, plays shortstop for the team."

"You know what those are?"

"I think I heard tell of them." He picks up the packet. "These what they call rubbers?"

"That or condoms," I say. "It's what you call protection in case you and this Juana fall in love, or, more likely, in bed.

"I said I wasn't going to give you advice unless you wanted it. You want it?"

"Yes, sir."

I crumple the wrappers and stuff them into the bag. Then I place my arms on the table and interlock my hands.

"I'm sure Juana is a fine girl," I say. "You and her may fall in love and raise a passel of young 'uns, and live happily ever after, but that needs to be 'cause you want to and not because you have to. You had better make sure she doesn't get pregnant. If you and her stay together, it needs to be 'cause y'all want to and not 'cause you have to. See what I'm saying?"

"It ain't like that."

"Good."

"She's going to college in the fall, she say."

"You know who Disney McLeod is?" I ask.

"No."

"She's Ryne Standback's gal. She was going to college in the fall, too. Now I'd bet my first paycheck she's living down near Corpus Christi in an oceanfront condo, Ryne rented with his bonus money. I met her mama when I was scouting Standback. She tried to get him arrested to prevent Ryne from running off with her daughter. Since he's in Corpus Christi and not in jail, I figure she didn't succeed, and she's living with him. Which is fine, but, as I said, you need to make sure that's what you want. The better you do, Taiquon, the more she's gonna love you. I've had a little experience in this area, a long time ago. Back then, I didn't know what I know now."

I decide to leave it at that.

My chief worry has been that Taiquon has too much to learn, as much about life as baseball, and plenty about both. Now he's flashing ahead like a runaway comet and hasn't donned a pair of cleats yet. I should've watched what I asked for. I might just get it.

Seldom have I seen a more motley crew than the one that showed up at the Buckhead Community College baseball stadium, which is also home of the Bucks. These boys like to party, and I think that's what they were doing all night if not this morning. They're dragging, every one of them except Taiquon, who seems to have reacted well to his morning bike ride. I wonder if the other players ever left Dreighton Parker's ranch. Things pick up once they get some sweat circulating.

When batting practice starts, the balls hit fair are few and far between. The shortstop I assume to be Juana's brother, Jesus Garcia, is as wild as the rest. It's hard for a righthanded batter to foul off a ball to the left. Garcia gets wood – this league uses such bats, which appeals to me – on a ball that otherwise would have hit him in the ribs. He somehow misses the front of the cage and lines it on a sharp curve into the empty third-base dugout. It would be a wonderful means of self-defense if he could do it on purpose.

He starts laughing.

"Trick-shot artist, homes," he says.

"You turned for real," one of his buddies says.

It's hard to identify flaws at batting-practice speed, but I try to watch the hijinks closely. I take a turn at throwing B.P., and like every position player who ever spent a decade or more in the bigs, I occasionally mix in my mediocre knuckleball, which none of them can hit. After about an hour, I see that, in their right minds, they're all pretty good athletes. After the pitching coach replaces me on the mound, Charlie Gabbard trots over to join me in the general area of the first-base coach's box.

"Whatcha think?" he asks.

"When this shindig started, I figured they all quit slugging down pitchers of beer about a half hour before they showed up," I say.

"I doubt that," he says, "but they're a happy-go-lucky bunch. It usually takes 'em a while to get going. It was the same way last year, and we wound up winning the league."

"You're the boss, Charlie. Just let me know what you want, and I'll try to do it."

"How you think your boy would do in the outfield?" he asks.

"I don't think he's got any experience except catcher and pitcher, and he didn't start pitching until late in the high school season," I reply, "but I don't think his future's at catcher. He's got too much speed to get worn down squatting behind the plate. I had the infield in mind, but he ought to make a pretty fair outfielder. He's got the tools."

"We got a good catcher," Charlie says. "I coach the college team, and he plays for me there, too. And our infield's fairly set, too."

"This is the same thing that happened to Taiquon at the state all-star game," I say. "The catcher was the coach's son. It surprised the hell out of me when he put Taiquon in to pitch. He did all right, though."

"Tell you what, Clyde. See if you can teach your boy how to play center field."

"I'll do what I can. The glove I bought him is for infielders, but I'll fix that in the morning."

"You bought his glove?"

"Till I came along, he didn't own one," I say. "That's how he became a catcher. If a poor kid plays catcher, the team supplies the mitt."

"No shit?" Charlie asks.

"No shit," I reply.

It's hot as hell on the field, and I wish I'd drunk some water before I went out there. Taiquon and I just talk, and when somebody hits a fly ball, Taiquon shags it with relative ease. I tell him the advantage of playing center field is that you can see the catcher's signals. Play the batter a little more to pull when a breaking ball is coming. Shade a few steps to the right field if the pitcher's got a good heater. It's just playing the percentages. Once the games start, I tell him to keep an eye on me in the dugout, and I'll send him signals on how to position himself. I tell him the most important job is to hit the cutoff man. Another advantage to center field, I say, is that the ball is less likely to curve toward the foul lines when it's hit to center. He's just got more ground to cover.

Taiquon isn't going to have much trouble becoming a competent outfielder. He runs down fly balls without hesitation. He'll have to learn a heap of little things to make him a fine one.

"What's that thing you was throwing every now and then?" Taiquon asks.

"That's a knuckleball. You try to let it loose without any spin, and the wind takes it whichever way it wants to go."

"The bottom fell out of the one you th'owed me," he says.

"That's the plan. If a knuckleball doesn't knuckle, it gets hit about four hundred feet. I think throwing one might have made me a little better at hitting one. If you're expecting one, and you hardly see folks throwing them no more, choke up on the bat and just try to get the bat on it. If a knuckleballer gets behind in the count, he's gonna have to throw a fastball, and if he had a good one, he wouldn't be throwing no knuckler. That's when you wear his ass out."

I feel better about Taiquon. He looks good hitting. I hope he'll stay away from his teammates and that sangria wine. I wouldn't mind it if Juana Garcia found another young ballplayer to chase.

CHAPTER 18

Game Week

The first game is Saturday night at home. By Friday morning, Taiquon has his very own Texas driver's license. It turns out that in Texas – and everywhere else, for all I know – an eighteen-year-old only has to make his multiple choices in something similar to a voting machine, the way Taiquon describes it, and then pass the supervised driving test. Late every morning, Juana picks him up, and I assume he takes the wheel of her tiny import and they drive around the back roads near the lake. He shows me his license Friday morning. I don't have to lift a finger or raise my voice. He is prouder, I think, of learning how to parallel-park than he is of learning how to play the outfield.

Juana picks him up, and he returns with a white Pontiac Grand Am that I estimate to be about twenty years old. Taiquon insists on taking me for a ride. He says one of Dray Parker's associates has helped him acquire liability insurance. I check the glove compartment and find a dog-eared owner's manual, registration, and proof of insurance. I tell him not to let his guard down because it's easy to develop a false sense of security out there on the road. The tires have a fair amount of tread left. It runs well. The brakes seem to work, and I don't detect any unusual noises. The engine clicks a little when it's idling, but I reckon it's about as sound as a twenty-year-old Pontiac can be.

On the week of the season opener, no one seems particularly anxious about being ready. Practice is about the same every day. It starts out lackadaisical and gets a little better once all the players work up a sweat. Charlie and I decide on how to split up the squad for a practice game. We go six innings, and each team

119

puts two pitchers on the hill for three apiece. Charlie manages one team.

The two players who live in the other half of the duplex are pitchers, one righty and one lefty. The one who came out on the deck of the duplex briefly is the lefty, a tall, goofy kid named Paul Hughie who obviously, in the sunshine, isn't Hispanic, after all. The righthander, Gleason Tolson, looks like a fair hitter, and it comes in handy because we don't have enough players on the split squads to use a designated hitter. Tolson is the opening-game starter, so he plays right field for my team. Hughie starts on the mound for Gabbard's bunch.

Because of the window fan that is frequently slotted in and out of the window next to the porch, it occurs to me that Hughie and Tolson might use it, sucking air outward, when one or both of them is smoking pot. I don't much care. The reason I'm here is Taiquon. Back in the day, it wasn't unusual for players to cop a buzz before spring training games. I did it occasionally when I knew I wasn't starting. Kids don't realize that their coaches, or parents, were once young themselves. Mainly they think we're all stupid or, worse, naive. Of course, I might be wrong. I might be stupid, but I've been around.

I'm trying to teach Taiquon stuff he doesn't know. I give him a bunt sign, knowing that, given his value to the Vosbrinck High School offense, he's probably never laid one down except in batting practice. His eyes get big and round when he sees my sign, and I have to nod to make sure he knows that, yes, I want him to bunt Jesus Garcia over with none out and the score tied in the fourth. I see the first-base coach, a black kid named Antwine Renfro, whispering to Garcia. They've got their doubts about Taiquon being able to get a bunt down, and they're right. Hughie might've noticed all this – me nodding, Renfro whispering – and he throws a high, hard one that Taiquon pops up to the catcher. Next time I'm pitching B.P., I'm going to make Taiquon bunt a few knucklers. In the meanwhile, I'll tell him to let the high ones pass if he's supposed to bunt. I make it up to Jesus by giving him the steal sign, and he winds up scoring on a two-out double by our third baseman, Josh Mizell, because he's running on the pitch.

Taiquon slaps a solid single in the fifth, driving in two, and we win, 6-4. The team is better than I expected. They know how to play the game, which is more than I can say for Taiquon. I guess he doesn't mind nicknames anymore because everybody, but Charlie and I are now calling him Ty. I stick with Taiquon; Charlie calls him "Wattsy."

I'm gratified that, after a week of practice, the players seem to accept and like Taiquon. Most are two or three years older. The chief exception is the lefthanded, power-hitting first baseman, who looks like a younger version of the actor Forest Whitaker. Jeremiah Sisler is twenty-five and a good ballplayer, slow of foot but slick around the bag. I wonder why he's not in pro ball. He looks about Double-A level to me.

Charlie calls him "Junior," so I reckon he must have a daddy.

In the short run, it's kind of nice around the house to have Taiquon occupied. I'm happy with the progress he's making on the field. The progress he's making socially is a bit troubling, but it's inevitable. I underestimated him. Hell, maybe I *should've* just signed him to a free-agent contract. Maybe he can fend for himself.

Frank Staley Jr. calls and apologizes for not keeping in touch better. He says the first-round draft pick, the pitcher, has been assigned to Rookie League in Montana. I share my feelings that Taiquon is doing better than I expected.

"I'll sign him any time you say," Frank says.

"We haven't even played a game," I say. "He's just better in the outfield than I thought. The talent level's decent, at least on this team, but he needs to face game competition. All the players are older than he is, and that's good in a way and bad in a way."

"Meaning?"

"I just worry that they're gonna be a bad influence. Everybody seems to like him. It's not good for a kid to hang out with people who are older. When I was with the Loggers, we had the nicest kid in the world, our batboy. Twelve years old. He was a rookie when I was. By the time he was eighteen, he was the clubhouse boy, street-smart, a hustler. Half the team was buying weed from him."

"Dylan Housel? That kid?"

"I really shouldn't say."

"He's working in the Oakland front office now," Frank says.

"Being clubhouse boy in Portland was probably good training for a big-league front office," I say.

"You don't need my advice. Look out for him."

"Did I mention he's got a girlfriend? And a driver's license. And a loaner to drive around in that Dray Parker, the owner, provided from one of his used-car lots."

"That was bound to happen, sooner or later," Frank says.

"At least he doesn't have much money," I say.

"Yeah. The root of all evil," Frank says. "You asked for this. I'm confident you're up to the task."

"It'd be a lot better if I didn't remember me at his age."

I tell him I'll call again in a day or two. Even though it's hot enough to imitate Death Valley, something possesses me to take the rowboat out into the lake. I work up a good sweat. I just drop the paddles in the floor and drift around for a while, thinking. Thank God I took my little Eskimo cooler along. I sip one of the two Diet Dr. Peppers I buried in ice from the freezer. I only drink bottled water when it's free.

Before I row my way back in, I call Ophelia just to let her know everything's fine with her grandboy.

I've got two more hours to kill before it's time to go to practice. I fix myself a couple turkey sandwiches, slather on some mayonnaise, coat the turkey with pepper, shake some chips onto the plate, add a dill pickle spear, and walk out on the porch with a glass of milk.

Gleason Tolson, the righty who is the opening-night starter, walks out on his side of the porch. I get up and unlatch the screen door between them and say, "Come on over. Let's shoot the shit."

"I'll be right back," he says, and returns with one of those energy drinks, Monster, I think. It's got what looks like fluorescent green claws on a black can, and my suspicion is that it tastes like it looks.

He sits in a wicker chair and pops the top. He's a nice-looking kid, stout, powerful, with sandy brown hair.

"I'm guessing you've been around," I say. "Tell me about the Edgewood Tomcats."

They're the first opponent.

"They're kind of built to play a certain way," he says. "They'll work you to death, I mean, a pitcher. None of 'em is what you'd call a free swinger. They're right well-coached. We won the league, but they beat me the only time I faced 'em. My aim is get ahead in the count."

"Mainly take a strike to start out with?"

"Yep."

"How's the control on your breaking ball?"

"I can get it over," he says.

"You throw a curve and a slider both?" I ask.

"Yep." We're obviously on a "yep," not "yes, sir," basis.

"If you think it's safe to throw the first one right down the pipe, do it with the curve," I say. "If what you say is still true, most of their hitters are going to swing at a fastball if they swing at all. You got a decent heater. If you get the call on the curve, follow it up with a four-seamer up, top edge of the strike zone or a little out of it, and set if you can get him to go after it. Then go to the slider, particularly if he's righthanded. If they're gonna work the count, you gotta be around the strike zone."

"Yep," he says, "but mine's a two-seamer."

"Then aim it higher," I say.

Gleason's wearing a tee shirt with a pocket. He pulls one of those Juul things out of it.

"Mind if I hit this?" he asks. "It ain't nothing but vapor."

"I don't care," I say. "Same thing I tell Taiquon. I ain't your daddy."

He takes what I understand they call a rip. He's right. The cloud quickly dissipates.

"I know it's probably bad for you," he says. "I bet cigarettes are five times worse. It relaxes me. When I'm pitching, I slip down the runway and hit it. Pisses me off when we play somewhere they ain't no runway."

"I had a manager who cupped a cigarette right there in the dugout," I say. "Jock Burley with the Loggers. That kind of went away when TV started showing more shots of the dugout. A few players smoked in the clubhouse, some of them while they were talking to the writers if there weren't no TV cameras around. Different age. I never did, but when you get to be my age, every time you hear about all the things that are bad for you, I remember, deep down, that they weren't no worse twenty years ago."

Gleason obviously doesn't mind too much me knowing.

"I don't 'juul' all the time," he says.

"Just when you're high?"

"I don't get high on game days."

"Hell, don't mind me," I say. "I just want you and Hughie to know I wasn't born yesterday. I'm just out here to develop a ballplayer. I'd appreciate it if you'd go easy on Taiquon. He ain't but eighteen, and he's lived a sheltered life. He grew up on the border between South Carolina and Georgia, and he hadn't ever been to Atlanta till we drove through. Raised by his grandmother. He's gonna grow up, but I don't want him to grow up too fast. Know what I mean?"

"Yep," Gleason says.

It feels a little strange, driving down to Buckhead without Taiquon in the passenger seat. He's got his own wheels. It might not be the worst thing if he falls on his ass to start out the season.

CHAPTER 19
Playing a Trick

I'm encouraged when the lovelorn center fielder, Taiquon Wattson, shows up at the ballpark shortly after I do. I'm sitting alone in the dugout, fiddling with my cell, reading about the latest Loggers game, when he ambles into the dugout, backpack on, a pair of wooden bats in sleeves, handles up, looking like some kind of otherworldly radio antennae, built to withstand high impact, or at least that's my weird fantasy. The opening game is three hours away. We're the only ones here, both uniformed. Taiquon sits down without saying anything.

"Why seventeen?" I ask, noting his number.

"What they gave me," he replies. "I don't have no preference."

"I'm good with numbers," I say. "I expect I could tell you what every player on my high school football team wore."

"What number you wear?" he asks for no good reason, just curiosity.

"Sixty-four in football," I say. "I was a pulling guard. In baseball, I was eight in Portland and Toronto, high school, too, for that matter. I couldn't be eight in Boston. It's retired there."

"Who wore it?"

"Carl Yastrzemski. Yaz."

I could have said Jack Benny, and Taiquon wouldn't have known any different.

"He's in the Hall of Fame," I say. "I took eighteen instead. When I was in grade school, Felix Millan wore seventeen for the Braves. The best seventeen was probably Denny McLain."

"Who?" Taiquon asks.

"He was the last pitcher to win thirty games."

"Oh, wow."

"What else is on your mind?" I ask.

He sits silent again for ten seconds that seemed like thirty.

"You was right, what you said about girls."

"Refresh my memory," I say.

"You said to make sure I don't let no girl say what I do."

I put my phone away.

"Juana's not pregnant?"

"Oh, no, no, nothing like that," he says. "I'm just feeling a little trapped, you know. She be getting where she wants to rule my life."

"That doesn't make her necessarily different from most of the women I've ever known. I got two exes I don't hardly ever talk to no more. It's hard to split with a woman and still be friends. I reckon that probably ain't changed."

"I don't understand women," he says.

"Don't feel so all alone," I reply, and then, by tacit agreement, I change the subject.

"You be careful driving, Taiquon. I know you've picked it up just fine, but, once you've been driving for a while, a lot of things get to be second nature. Until then, you gotta keep your mind on the road when you're running around."

"Yes, sir."

"When I first got my daytime license, I was fifteen, and my dad decided I should take everybody to school in the morning. I'm the oldest. I was in high school, and I had to take my brother to junior high – I think they call that middle school now – and my sister to elementary school. One day my dad's car was in the shop, and the dealership gave him a loaner. It was a white Dodge, a big four-door sedan. I still remember it had a blue interior. Between grade school and junior high, I pulled out in front of somebody at a stop sign, and the other car hit me in the left-front fender. It wasn't a big deal, other than Daddy screaming at me when he found out. The dealership had insurance on it, but there was a problem with me being that young. Dad pulled a few strings with the cop – he got there about five minutes after it happened – got himself listed as the driver. I don't believe neither one of us ever said a word about it again. I must've learned something. I ain't never had a wreck in all the years since. What I'm trying to say is, whether it's a cute little gal or an automobile, you gotta learn from your mistakes, know what I mean?"

"Yes, sir," Taiquon replies. "I know exactly what you mean."

It's Opening Night. I think somebody wrote a book called *Why Life Begins on Opening Day*. It doesn't seen so profound to me anymore. I reckon I've had too many. After I complete my stint throwing batting practice, I retire to the dugout to sit down and think. Ponder my station in life, that sort of thing. The only other guy there is Jeremiah "Junior" Sisler, the hulking first baseman who, because Charlie Gabbard has penciled his name on the lineup card at designated hitter, feels no obligation to field a few grounders like every other first baseman/DH I've ever known, including myself late in my career. The time-honored traditions are dying away, I reckon, but it's not my place to say, Charlie being in charge and all. Junior's just dying for me to say something, but I keep my peace until he slides a little closer on the bench, and I figure he's determined to pick a fight.

"Clyde," he says, making me realize that we are on a first-name basis. "Clyde, no shit, what are you even doing here?"

"I could pose the same thing to you, Junior. You've got a lot of skills. How come you aren't playing professionally somewhere?" At least my question is complimentary.

"How do you know I haven't?"

"I don't," I reply. "That's why I asked. If it's not my business, just don't answer."

"I got sidetracked."

I leave it at that, but he doesn't.

"I make a good living working with Mr. Parker," he says. I notice he says *with*, not for. Again, I don't say anything.

.."Plus, I like playing ball."

"Sounds like you've got a pretty good life then," I say.

"Damn straight," he says. "Getting back to the question I had. You never answered. What are you doing here?"

"I'm trying to make a ballplayer out of Taiquon," I say. "I didn't think it was a secret."

"Why didn't you just sign the boy and learn all that shit in the minors?"

"Well, the secret is that nobody but me and a friend in the Loggers' front office knows about him. He's eighteen in age and a whole lot younger than that in life. He ain't ready for pro ball. When he is, if he is, I'll try to make that happen."

"You do this all the time?" Junior asks.

"Nope," I say. "First time."

"What's that mean?"

"It means I think he can be something special. I think he needs me around to protect him."

"What's in it for you?"

"Probably not enough to really make it worth the time," I say. "I reckon I want to prove my detractors wrong. Everything in the bigs has got modern. I want to prove it can still be done the old way."

"Just let me be," Junior says.

I turn toward him. "Junior, hypothetically, if you come up, and there's a man on first with none away, and you get a bunt sign, you gonna lay one down?"

"No way in hell."

"Good to know," I say.

The Edgewood Tomcats start a southpaw with a decent hitter. We go up and down in the first and second innings. Taiquon is batting seventh, so he leads off the bottom of the third, us trailing 1-0. Gleason Tolson looks pretty good, too. His curve is working, and he stays ahead in the count.

I tell Taiquon that the righty is going to try to get ahead of him, so he's going to throw a fastball right down the middle on the opening pitch. If I'm right, I tell him not to worry about a take sign from Charlie. Knock the hell out off it. Taiquon follows orders. He hits his first pitch in the North Texas Independent League over the fence in left-center. A happy boy slaps my hand as he rounds first base.

That sets off a rally. We score three more runs on a double, a one-out single, a triple, and a ground-ball out. The inning ends when Junior Sisler hits a mile-high fly ball to the track that the Edgewood right fielder barely catches. The only sign Charlie Gabbard gave was the "take" that Taiquon ignored.

Taiquon makes a diving catch in the sixth, but the Tomcats threaten in the seventh. The leadoff batter triples into the left-field corner, though I expect it would have been a double if Jayden Lorenzen hadn't fiddled around with the ball after first losing it in the lights. Gleason is shaken and walks the next batter. Taking advantage of my newfound reputation as a man of great athletic smell, I ask Charlie to let me make a trip to the mound for him. I wonder if the first base coach is allowed to counsel a pitcher.

I motion for the infielders to join me and Gleason on the mound. They all wear looks that say what in hell am I doing out there? I ignore them.

I tell Gleason the shifty Latino on third is going to try to steal the plate.

"Why do you think that?"

"'Cause I notice you still take your sweet time even when you're in the stretch, and you're probably not going to pay any attention to him with a man on first," I say. "I wouldn't be surprised if he broke for the plate when you throw to first."

"What do you want me to do?" Gleason asks.

"Go to the windup," I say. "Act like you forgot there's a man on first."

"Are you crazy?"

"Might be, but here's what I think is going to happen. You pitch from the windup, and it's damned near an automatic double steal." I turn toward the catcher, Oleo Culbertson. "I want you to throw through but not to the bag. Jesus (that's the shortstop, not Christ), even though the batter is righthanded, I want you to cover the bag. Reggie (Dunbar, the second baseman), I want you to take the throw behind the mound, and yank it to third."

"Why not the plate?" he asks.

"Because," I say, "the baserunner, until the ball goes through, isn't going to break for the plate, but he'll stray far enough off third that he'll be dead meat. Gleason, throw a fastball high, out of the zone, to give Oleo a good throwing angle, then duck. If I'm wrong, and the kid at third breaks right away, yell 'plate.' Otherwise, Reggie, you throw it to third."

The plate umpire strolls out to shut down the conference.

"Got it?" I ask, and everybody nods.

It's just like instant potatoes. Just add water. We nail the kid at third, Gleason straightens out, and we get out of the inning.

Paul Hughie comes in to pitch the last two innings, and we win, 6-1. Taiquon goes three-for-four, adding two singles. In the bottom of the eighth, he strikes out when a side-arm reliever gets him to lunge at a slider in the dirt on a full count. He'll learn that lesson next.

CHAPTER 20
Small World

In the absence of Taiquon Wattson, who expends a small part of his inexhaustible energy motoring around the countryside in the company of Juana Garcia or some newfound beauty, I've given up my homebody tendencies. I've gotten into the habit of having breakfast each morning at a popular cafe about four miles away at a Lake Texoma marina. I'm fond of a big breakfast and a moderate dinner, with nothing in between, except maybe a pack of crackers and a pint of chocolate milk. I'm getting my exercise at the ballpark. When I get up, I have a cup of coffee, shave (maybe), take a quick shower, and head over to Clyde's Cafe, which is owned by a man whose last name, unlike mine, is Clyde. I met Perry Clyde once, but he's usually not around during the breakfast hours.

What brings me there most mornings is the option of grits with eggs, bacon, and, if I'm feeling a bit Texan, chicken-fried steak with white gravy. We call it "sweet-milk" gravy back home. Then there's Rosie, the waitress with a heart of gold. They don't hire waitresses like Rosie at Applebee's. She's gorgeous for, oh, forty-five, maybe, laughs easily and often at herself, and has no visible attachment in the form of a ring. She unquestionably has me lusting in my heart, but the two of us haven't gotten friendly enough for me to know so much as her last name. It's competitive. Every man in there – most are going out to fish – is in love with Rosie to some extent or another. To this point, no one seems to recognize me as a former ballplayer. Rosie knows I coach baseball, but she doesn't seem to be a particular fan. I made enough of an impression for her to ask why I do it, and I replied by telling her I'm retired and do it just for fun, which is not entirely untrue. I hope she thinks I made my "fortune" selling real estate.

"I know your kind," she says one morning. "You just want to go back to being young again."

"There's no change," I reply. "I've always been that way. How about you?"

"Got neither the money nor the time," she says. "Too many mouths to feed. Too many young'uns to watch."

"I got that last thing in common. You gotta watch these kids like a hawk on rabbits. The good thing is they all think I'm stupid. They don't realize I was young once, too."

"My son still plays baseball," Rosie says, "and my daughter spends all her time following his team around. I think she chases all the boys."

Oh, surely not.

"I don't suppose your son's name is Jesus Garcia?"

"I already knew the world around here was small," the apparent Rosie Garcia says. "So you coach the Bucks?"

"Assistant," I reply. "My personal interest is in a young man named Taiquon Wattson. I'm guessing you've met him."

"He seems like a sweet boy," she says. "Juanita loves him to death."

"From time to time, it might not be a bad idea for us to compare notes," I say.

It is the most unusual pickup line I have ever uttered.

The general pattern of the Buckhead Bucks' schedule is to play games on Mondays, Wednesdays, Fridays, and Saturdays. The college allows us unlimited use of the field, and Dreighton Parker pays the same grounds crew that works the college games to keep it up for ours. Charlie Gabbard, who manages the team, also runs the ballpark, though Junior Sisler, of all people, allegedly runs the concessions. Charlie says the money he makes from the ballclub makes up for the money he used to make by conducting summer camps. The team has a decent fan base. I'd guess we're averaging three hundred fans during the week and four or five hundred on weekends, though that may wind up being a bit high once the novelty of the opening games wears off. The fans are mostly very young or very old.

Three games in, we haven't come close to losing. The fact that Taiquon is hitting over .400 has been noted by the local weekly, whose young writer interviewed him and me after Taiquon cleared the bases with a double to break open a 9-4 win over the Braun Buffaloes on Monday night. I doubt a story in the *Buckhead Banner* is going to be picked up by the Associated Press.

On Wednesday, we all board our old bus, which I believe once rode the country's Continental Trailways, for a forty-mile trip across the Red River into Oklahoma to play the Washita Braves. The forecast calls for scattered showers, and I'm hoping we can get the game in and not have to return the following night. This is both for obvious reasons – I don't have any particular love of bus rides – and the fact that Rosie Garcia has Thursday night off, and we've made tentative plans to meet for dinner.

It's a roomy bus, and it seems to run well. Charlie drives it. I sit behind him, and the pitching coach, Harvey Spice, is across the aisle. Perhaps because he is retired Army, but I imagine also because his name otherwise sounds as if he's part of a gay chorus, Harvey goes by "Sarge." The middle rows are sparsely populated by a few stray players who spend all their time texting, but most of the better players crowd the back, undoubtedly so that they can ridicule the rest of us with presumed security.

Taiquon has been accepted. He is in the very back row. This pleases me but also makes me a bit uneasy. His naive sense of humor amuses the others. I hadn't noticed a sense of humor in the long drive trip from South Carolina.

I sense a little resentment in Sarge, probably because I made the mound visit in the opener to set up the trick play that got us out of an Edgewood threat. He can't really say much because it worked, but there's a mild rub between us that's left unsaid. Antwine Renfro, who is both player and coach, begins the trip up front, listening to music on what is apparently known as earbuds, but later he drifts to the back, dividing time between his roles. I expect they probably chide him for being a spy.

We're going to get the game in. I feel it in my bones. I think my sense of destiny is returning. When I was a kid, I expected to succeed. I fulfilled my aspirations. I thought it was more than what I deserved. I came to believe I was destined to succeed at everything. It wasn't religious in nature, but it could have been. I never could bring myself to believe God was a fan, and that, somehow, by me hitting a baseball, He had decided I was some sort of golden boy. I did, however, think I was a golden boy, too, and I also didn't buy the arrogance that I was good at hitting a ball because I worked harder than anyone else. I thought it immodest to give myself such credit.

Anyway, when I got older, and, occasionally, I couldn't will myself to glory anymore, and when I failed at things – things like marriages and families and job applications – it started chinking the armor of destiny. All of a sudden, things didn't work after a lifetime of things working.

Now, what do you know? Taiquon falls into my lap. I think I'm going to make something big of him. He's got the tools. I've got the polish. I'm worried about what this cute little Juana is going to do to him because cute little Juanas used to do things to me, and what do you know again? I'm falling in love with Juana's mother, and it's an absolute accident.

The stardust of destiny is wafting about.

Taiquon has his first rough night of the season. He goes oh-for-three, walks, and gets thrown out stealing. Puddles in the outfield befuddle him. He makes no errors but messes up a throw because his right foot slid out from under him when he was trying to hit the cutoff man. No error is charged, but we'd have thrown out the runner at the plate if the cutoff had been exercised. The guy scored from first on a double that should have been a single. We win anyway, 4-2. We only had three hits. One of them was a Junior Sisler grand slam.

I think it's good for him. He needed to be knocked down a peg. What disappoints me is that he doesn't seek me out afterward. He asks me if it's all right to talk in the morning. I reminded him that I'm not his daddy, and that I'm not going to tell him what to do. He wants to ride home with Juana Garcia. I'm guessing their tiff has run its course. Most of the players ride home with their girlfriends. Apparently, it's important to Charlie Gabbard that everyone rides the bus to the game, but he doesn't care how they get home. It's just a half hour. One of these nights, a kid's going to get killed in a car wreck, or kill someone else, or get busted for simple possession, and that's when everyone's going to have to ride the bus home again. I hope that day is when I'm no longer out here.

All our players are good for this level. Junior and Taiquon are the two with talent above the rest. I'm aching to know the whole story about Junior. I reckon I'll get it in bits and pieces over the next few weeks. A part of me is beginning to think my work here is done. Taiquon is adapting faster than I thought possible. He doesn't say "yes, sir" all the time anymore.

I decided to dedicate myself to patching up things with Sarge Spice. I sit across the aisle from him. With the bus three-quarters entry, it doesn't make sense to sit side-by-side.

"Sarge, when I went out to the mound and put that trick play together, it was stupid in any other situation and in any other game but the first one of the year," I say.

"It worked," he replies. "That's all that matters."

"I just wanted you to know I'm not trying to take over."

I reckon that's about it. Not much more for me to say. Not much more for Sarge to say. If there's any wind, it'll blow over.

I'm up early on Thursday morning. When I leave the cabin, I don't know whether Taiquon came in last night or not. The white Pontiac isn't at the house. Juana could've dropped him off. If so, she'll come to get him later. The team has no practice. I vaguely figure the odds are that he spent the night with her. The bottom line is that I don't care. It's one more reason to spend some time with Rosie, but my intentions are not altogether professional.

"The boys won a close one, I hear," she says when I take a seat on a stool at the counter.

Business is slow.

"Be good for 'em," I say.

"How's Taiquon?"

"He wasn't up when I left. Last night's first game he didn't get a hit. I reckon he's a little down on himself."

"Jesus was up early," she says. "That's unusual. He wanted to tell me how well he played."

"He looked good," I reply. "I reckon I'll have the usual."

"I'm guessing that's bacon and sausage both. Grits and two eggs, over-medium. Sourdough toast?"

"You got it."

Jesus is a decent ballplayer, but he takes too long to throw to be a shortstop. He has to cock before he throws. We don't turn many double plays. He's a good fastball hitter, though, especially for a kid who grew up with aluminum bats. He's pretty good at getting wood on the ball and hitting the ball where it's pitched. That's one of those baseball terms that doesn't make much sense literally. He pulls inside pitches, hits one down the middle where it comes from, and slices outside pitches to right. He probably does that better than anyone else on the team, including Taiquon. There's no reason to tell his mother any of this.

"You still on for tonight?" I ask.

"Yeah. Where do you want to go?"

"You're the one who lives here. Suits me wherever you say?"

"You like fish?" she asks.

"Love 'em."

"Meet me at Jernigan's. It's on the Sherman Highway, about halfway between here and there. I'll meet you at seven."

"Sounds like a plan," I say. "I've seen the place."

CHAPTER 21

Off to Another Beaten Path

It's a shame I have only one date with Rosie Garcia. She's charming. So is Jernigan's, a cafe whose tables have red-and-white checkerboard cloths and whose waitresses wear dresses made of gingham. The food is spicy and Cajun-influenced. I order catfish because it is familiar and I know it to be tasty. It comes with red beans and rice and corn on the cob. Rosie orders jambalaya, and it makes me envious. She has looked me up and knows I once played and managed a major league baseball team. I have to specifically confess why I am here. Now we both have ulterior motives. I am protective of Taiquon, and she wants to know if I can help her son. I don't tell her I can't, but she probably gets the correct impression. I say he is mismatched by position for pro ball, that he might make a second baseman, or a third baseman, or an outfielder, but not a shortstop.

This dampens the conversation regarding baseball, which isn't necessarily bad. I still have the hots for her, and I'm getting to an age where the hots don't come along that often and are most often relegated to the realm of fantasy. I'm leery of romance, having failed miserably at it so many times. Failed romance has cost me about half of what I might otherwise be worth.

In a way, I guess that's fine. Stripped of our respective agendas, we have a good time. I tell her what it's like to live in my hometown, even though no one else in my family is still there. I talk about Taiquon, but not so much about him as a ballplayer, but how much the naivete has eroded since we arrived in Texas, and he joined a ballclub of players older than he and got a girlfriend, a car, and a license to drive it. I tell her he's putting his reliance on me behind, and it's probably not a bad thing. She says the same thing about Jesus and Juana, but, like Ophelia Sanders, she isn't altogether happy about it.

Rosie likes Shiner Bock, so we split a pitcher of it, and the buzz loosens up the conversation. We each drink the amount of beer it takes to serve as a truth serum.

"What do you think of Latino people?" she asks from out of nowhere.

"I think the same I think of all people," I reply. "People are people. We have different backgrounds and heritages, but that's what America is for."

"Have you ever been … involved with a Latino."

"Well, I've gone out with Latino people. I am not reluctant."

"What do you think would be the result of a black person who is involved with a Latino?"

Ah. It's not about me and her. It's about Taiquon and Juana. I take a deep breath.

"Okay," I say. "Here's what I think. I have never thought wrong, about interracial relationships or marriage, but, when I was younger, I worried about what others thought. The world has changed in our lifetime, and what I think is important now is that, let's say, in the case of Taiquon and your daughter, two people live at a higher level than ignorance."

"What do you mean by that?" She heats up a little and also pours herself another glass. I motion to the waitress that we'd like one more pitcher and buy a little time by finishing off my glass.

"I mean, let's just say that Taiquon and Juana fall deeply in love, if they haven't already, and they get married, or they move in together, and they have kids. If Taiquon becomes a big-league ballplayer and a celebrity, Juana raises money for charity, and they live comfortably in the suburbs, it will not be a problem. But if Taiquon ends up working in a warehouse, and they live in an apartment complex, they will live in an environment where people who are also less successful, uneducated, and more bigoted, then it will make their lives even more difficult. That's what I think. They are both taking a leap of faith, and a leap of love, and they probably don't realize it, and they won't believe it if either one of us tells them that."

"You're right," Rosie says. "Kids gotta make their own mistakes. God knows I did."

"Me, too. My trouble is I had to make those mistakes before I learned what I had done wrong," I say. "I have concluded that you can't tell a young'un nothing. The best you can hope is that he will ask you what you think. Then, and only then, will he, or she, listen to what you have to tell him. Or her."

"It's different for you, Rosie," I add. "Taiquon is not my son. My job is to fine-tune his skills as a baseball player. I do not, and will not, tell him what to do with his life. I'm amazed at how much he is changing, but I'm not going to tell him what he can't do as far as his life is concerned. I'll tell him what I think if he asks me, and he asks me quite a lot, but he doesn't ask me as much as he used to. I think it's kind of amazing how much he has learned, how much he has adapted. Honestly, I brought him to Texas because I didn't think he could make it on his own. I thought he needed help. Now I'm not so sure. I've taught him a lot about how to be a ballplayer, and how to play the game, but as a person, I don't think he needs anywhere near as much as I thought. It's almost like I've gotten more from him than he has from me."

"I'm glad you feel that way," Rosie says.

Then my phone rings. I meant to cut it off. It is Frank Staley Jr. I tell him I'll call him right back.

"I gotta take this," I say. "It's my friend, my semi-boss, my ally, with the Loggers. The guy who let me do this. I'm gonna step out on the porch. I'll cut it as short as I can."

I tell Frank Jr. to give me a second, pour myself a beer from the pitcher that just arrived, refill Rosie's glass for her, and leave her sitting there, considering what I just said.

I take a seat in a rocking chair on the porch, down at the end where no one is nearby. I take a decent-sized drink of the Shiner Bock, sit the glass on the rail, and gaze at the sunset. Then I call back.

"What's up, Frank? I'm kind of occupied. We're off tonight, and I'm out to dinner with a lady I met," I say.

"Good for you, Clyde. I'll try to be brief," Junior says, "but it's not gonna be easy. Quickly, how's Taiquon?"

"Couldn't be better. He's hitting over .400. Playing the hell out of the center field. The team is undefeated, and he's learned a whole lot off the field, too. I'm sure that couldn't be the sole purpose of this call."

"It's Ryne Standback," he says. "He wants to see you."

"Me? Kid can't stand me. Feeling's mutual. Why would he want to see me?"

"Well, I just found out about it secondhand. He called the scouting office and talked to Cliff Hueble. Hueble walks down the hall, ducks in my office – usually he summons me to his – and says Standback wants to talk to you."

"Again," I say, "why in the name of Dan Plesac would he want to talk to me?"

"I called him. He says you're the only person in baseball who's ever been truthful to him. I probably shouldn't have told him that you were in Texas, because then he said he had to see you. He wants you to come down to Corpus Christi. Says he needs your help badly, and it won't take but a day or two."

"And you told him that, unfortunately, that wasn't going to be possible."

"I would have," Frank says, "but there's more to it than that."

"There always is," I say. "Did I tell you that Taiquon and I watched Standback play a game in Frisco?"

"No."

"We got here a couple of days early. We had stopped several times to watch minor league games on the way out. I didn't even know Ryne was playing in Corpus Christi. As I expected, he looked way overmatched."

"At the moment," Frank says, "he's hitting a whopping .163."

"And?"

"As you know, Hueble and the rest of the scouting department wanted to draft him. The main reason they didn't, in addition to your recommendation and my taking your side, was the demands from his agent, who's an unreasonable nobody with a chip on his shoulder. Now they think they can make a deal for him as a throw-in with Covid Malloy for Xhi-Pe Quan.

"Malloy? Lefthanded pitcher, ain't he?"

"Yeah. He's a starter, up and down. Houston hasn't got room for him in the rotation. We need pitching help. They need an infielder who can play anywhere. Xhi-Pe is leading our club on average, but we need help in the rotation. Malloy's their fifth starter, at best. He'd be number two or three here. Apparently, Houston's soured on Standback already. Our guys want to develop him in Single-A, where he ought to be."

"Why ain't he there now?"

"Contract," Frank says. "If we take him, that's gonna have to change."

"Let me get back to Miss Rosie," I say, "if she ain't left in a huff already. I'll call you first thing in the morning."

I go back to the table thinking we might need a third pitcher of beer. I'm wrong. Rosie is ready to go home, and she came in her own car. I tell her I'm sorry as I pay the tab.

Over the years, my baseball skills wore out, but my ability to travel didn't. I can pack a bag in my sleep. I've had all the trials and made all the errors. All my bags are uncommon colors. Once I picked up a bag at the claim in Denver, went to pick up the rental car, hoisted the suitcase in the trunk, and realized it wasn't mine. I drug that suitcase back to the terminal — it was when I was managing in the minors – and there was my bag going around and around, and a man waiting for the one I was rolling. If he had been a larger man, he'd have likely whupped my ass, but he wasn't and didn't. I unzipped the suitcase, pulled a baseball out of it, autographed it, and asked if he was from Racine. I think that's where it was. He said he was, so I said I'd leave him a season pass for two at the club's ticket office. I was gone for a month to take over the club in Medicine Hat, Alberta.

First things first, and the departure winds up being smooth. I don't even see Taiquon, so I write him a note and place it on his bed in the unlikely event that he still sleeps there. Paul Hughie and Gleason Tolson know I'm taking a weekend trip before Taiquon does. I find Dreighton Parker at his office and tell him the big club is sending me on an errand. No problem, he says. The Loggers put a little money in the Bucks, and he's grateful for bringing Taiquon along if nothing else. He says me and the boy are making him money. Then I find Charlie Gabbard at the ballpark, working on the pitcher's mound, and he says have a good time and hurry back.

Corpus Christi is a place I've never been to, but I know it's a long way. The video screen in the truck tells me it will take seven hours, and two minutes, to get there by way of Dallas, Austin, and San Antonio. I learned a long time ago to avoid Dallas at all costs, so I redirect through Fort Worth, a global positioning satellite be damned, and I try to hit the cities when traffic isn't oppressive, but there are too many of those to achieve it. Thank God for satellite radio and an afternoon game from Wrigley Field. It doesn't make much sense on a Friday, but the game last night was rained out, and there's a day-night twin bill. A little bit shy of Waco, it occurs to me that giving Ryne Standback a call might be in order. I tell the onboard communications from General Motors to ring the number Frank Staley Jr. texted me, and I'm damned if I know what to expect.

I reckon Ryne answers because he sees it's a South Carolina number, even though I'm from "864" and he's from "803." He might have enough sense to suspect it is I, though I wouldn't bet on it.

"Uh, Mr. Kinlaw?"

"Ryne ... yup ... it's me," I say. "I can't imagine why you want to talk to me, but I'm on my way to Corpus Christi."

"Did Mr. Staley tell you what I told him?"

I'm amazed the Standback I know has the word "mister" in his vocabulary.

"Yeah. I wouldn't have believed it if it hadn't come from him," I say. "Frank Junior and I go back a long way. I knew his old man. The Hooks start at seven or thereabouts?"

"Yes, sir." Damn. He sounds like Taiquon used to.

"Well, I don't know if I can get there by the time the game starts, but I reckon I'll be there by the time it ends. I'll come down to the locker room then, and we'll talk then."

"I'll leave you a pass," he says.

"Don't need one, Ryne. I got one that works about everywhere. I saw you play in Frisco about three or four weeks ago."

"I appreciate you coming, Mr. Kinlaw."

"Call me Clyde. Mister ain't necessary. My kids don't even call me Daddy. They hardly call me at all. I'll see you, hear?"

I get the impression he wants to talk more right now, but that will have to wait. I need the highway to get some thinking done, so I politely say bye and wonder why Ryne Sandback, the arrogant jackass, has developed a taste for humble pie.

CHAPTER 22
Snap Back ... with Standback

$\mathcal{I}$ can't do without coffee. I see lots of truck stops – they prefer "travel center" in most cases nowadays – where I fill up on gas and coffee and relieve myself to make room for the next mug. I never even drank coffee until I was in my thirties. I think the reason I started was it was free in hotel rooms. Give me a steady supply of country music or a ballgame on satellite radio and global satellite positioning, and I can just about drive around the clock. Sometimes on a vacant four-lane at two in the morning, I'll play along with the radio on my harmonica. A man's got to keep his mind occupied.

That preoccupation helps me live day by day. I search for universal thoughts. I'm going to see Ryne Standback because he inexplicably wants to see me, and the Loggers are making it worth my time, and I'd just as soon make the slate as clean as I can. He seems like a changed man. Taiquon Wattson has made me a changed man, so I think I'll just pick up the story as if it were a brand-new one. Out of all my virtues and a few of my vices, my ability to just take what I see is my favorite. It's just that most of the world doesn't care for it. I just take what I see and figure out what I think. Others seem to be confused by what to me seems honest.

I'm fully formed, perhaps to my detriment. I am well past entertaining any fundamental change. I don't hold many grudges. I'm open to Standback changing my mind. I'm a little sorry that I've been so right about him.

I get hung up in Austin traffic but cruise around San Antonio with little irritation, switching at last from Interstate 35 to

37, which ends at Corpus Christi Bay. The woman's voice that directs me from the dash politely interrupts the music to keep me along my way. She's a little fussy when I stop from time to time.

Mild curiosity occupies me for a while as Corpus Christi draws near. I wonder how Taiquon will react to my absence. I hope not at all. Any time a kid starts to step out on his own, he changes. Inevitably, some good and some bad emerge. Taiquon has changed astonishingly. I hope he's got enough sense to stay out of trouble, particularly with those pot-smoking pitchers next door.

Naturally, I don't announce my presence after I check into a Hampton Inn and reach Whataburger Field, the orange-splashed home of the Hooks. Orange is favored by both the parent Astros and the sponsoring hamburger chain. I think about paying my way in, thus avoiding the pass gate, but because there is little sinister in my visit, that I'm tight with money and know I'll never remember to put ballpark admission on an expense form, and because some accountant will request an explanation, I use my pass card. Assuming naturally that I am a scout, the cheerful young woman behind the glass assigns my space behind the plate, where undoubtedly other scouts will congregate. It's possible that some enterprising employee of the club might recognize my name, but I doubt it.

I walk quickly away from my assigned area. I need a decent seat, but it's a Friday night crowd and I wind up down the right field, high rows, with modest space around me. I am wearing khaki shorts, a navy golf shirt, sunglasses, and a floppy, brown hemp hat. In short, I am like any other ex-ball player hoping not to be identified. I hate to be brusque, but it's hard to pay attention to the game with someone wanting to talk about that time I broke up Art Flannel's no-hitter with a game-winning blast.

Having no time to ask around about Ryne Standback's reputation with the faithful, and no intention of gossiping with other scouts, I just watch him play. I have only my small pair of binoculars and a notepad to scribble what little I am likely to forget. Standback looks much better around the bag. The Astros have straightened out his footwork. Good for them. I'm surprised they got him to listen.

At the plate, he's consistent. Consistently bad, from either side of the plate. He's got the same swing, probably a result of his daddy's money. He's had his swing analyzed so many times that he has achieved the recommended sameness. I don't know how many switch hitters have the same swing on both sides, as hard as coaches work to make that happen. Standback can't lay off a high fastball, and he's a sucker for a slider outside in the dirt. With that swing, he's bound to make a pitcher pay for a mistake, but he doesn't know how to wait for it. If he took more pitches and waited for a fastball, he'd hit a hundred points higher on those habits alone. He's a hacker, though, and that's a habit he didn't have in high school. I knew he was stubborn, but he was letting the frustrations consume him.

I never played much first base. I was an outfielder until the Astroturf of Toronto's Exhibition Stadium ruined both knees. I played a little first base at the end of the year in Canada, but Boston signed me as a designated hitter. I could always hit, but I decided to retire late one Saturday afternoon at Fenway. The manager of the Red Sox at the time often played his tactical cards too quickly, and he ran out of options that day and inserted me in the game as the right fielder, which is spacious at the Red Sox' home. I wasn't in the lineup to begin with because I was having a bad-knee day, and I limped out there and lined up about as deep as anyone had ever seen. It was the thirteenth inning, and the first two batters grounded out. I had to make the final out, and it should have been a homer, but I ran as fast as I could, which wasn't very, jumped a little at the bullpen wall, caught it, and then fell into the warning track with a considerable thud. I got an especially long-standing ovation because it took thirty seconds to get back to the dugout.

I finished out the season and waited until spring training so that the Loggers could sign me to a free-agent contract and I could retire where I had nine good years. Everything was arranged. I spent that summer as a roving batting instructor, then became the big club's first-base coach and two years later, the manager.

The ballpark is typical of so many. It's not brand-new, but it has a nice backdrop -- a bridge behind right field -- the fancy scoreboard, the goofy fan-participation contests between innings, and the people who must have something to do for every single minute while thumbing away at a cell phone at the same time.

By contemporary standards, this qualifies as charm.

Standback actually gets two hits, neither of which he deserves. Fooled and jammed on a change-up, bloops a sliced wedge into shallow left field in the sixth inning and takes advantage of a bobble in the hole by the Midland shortstop to reach in the eighth. Midland is the RockHounds. They won, 6-4.

In spite of my lack of preparation, I find the locker room exit easily and wait outside. Standback is about the fifth one out, eyes darting for a few seconds before they meet mine. He walks over, seeming cordial enough. I don't know what to expect.

"Did you make the game?" he asks.

"Walked in after two batters."

"I looked for you behind the plate."

"Ah, I found an empty seat," I say. "I wasn't in a mood to mingle with folks I might know."

"I worried that you wouldn't go to the trouble," Standback says. "I just want to say ..."

"Look," I interject, "let's not talk right here."

"Well, I just want to say that you saved my ass back home," he insists. "I know you don't like me, and you were probably right about that, but, but that was then, and I want to show you I've changed."

"That's all? That's why you wanted me to come all the way down here?"

"No, no," Standback says. "I just wanted to get that in right out front."

I tell him my room number at the Hampton and tell him to get there as soon as he can. I think of Rosie and stop at a convenience store to buy a six-pack of Shiner Bock. I walk down the hall to fill the ice bucket, jam three beers in it, and I'm about halfway through sipping my first when Standback shows up.

"Sit down, Ryne," I say.

He has a little zip-up bag. Fortunately, the room has two beds.

"Planning to sleep over?"

"I got nothing to do till late tomorrow afternoon," he says.

I sit in the recliner, and Sandberg sits down on the couch.

"I'll give you a beer if you'll trade me your keys," I say. "I know you're underage, and I know you drink anyway."

"How's that?"

"When I scout a player, I don't just scout him on the field," I answer. "How you think I knew your girlfriend's old lady was out to get you?"

"You saved my ass," Standback says. "Trouble is, I need you to save it again."

"Hang on," I say. "I think I need to cross the street and buy another six-pack."

CHAPTER 23
Girl Problems

My mind returns to the carefree minor-league days of yore, when men were men, played like hell all night, drank beer till dawn, slept all day, and started all over again. Sipping beer in a motel room is the old man's version. When I reached the bigs, ballplayers went out to bars in some cities and beer joints in others. By the time I was done, my younger teammates went to strip joints and made drug deals. I made friends by drinking beer with the manager and coaches. It probably made me a natural choice to manage and coach.

A six apiece of Shiner and a sink full of ice is perfect for me and Ryne Standback, a repentant young man who has to tell me details he'd rather hide. Beer helps, I think. It has an aspect of truth serum to it. I expect Ryne will stop hemming and hawing about three beers in.

"This beer tastes good," he says. "I haven't had one in going on three weeks now."

"Oh?"

"My roommate's a Mormon," he says. "Trust me. I'll get to that later."

There's no need to get off on a tangent. I might forget to tell him something he needs to know.

"One of your problems," I say, "are you trying to pull everything, and there are lots of pitches you can't pull. You being able to hit the opposite field, at least on purpose, is gonna take a lot of work. That's not for me. I've already got a project for that."

"Why are you out here?"

"I'm making a ballplayer out of Taiquon Wattson. Remember him?"

"The catcher from Vosbrinck?"

"He's a semi-pro center fielder in Buckhead now," I reply. "Buckhead, Texas."

"I'd say you got quite a job," Ryne says.

"He's coming along, but I didn't drive all the way down here to talk about Taiquon. This trip is about you. If you take a smart approach to hit, you can do all right here, for a while, anyway. You need to work at a lower level, but there are two pitches you can't hit, and you need to minimize your swings at high fastballs and breaking balls away. Even at this level, lots of pitchers try to get ahead in the count by opening with a fastball right down the middle. You go up to the plate laying for that. I'm not talking about a high one. You can lay off that thing. Don't swing at a first-pitch-breaking ball. If the pitcher opens with a curveball or a slider, let it pass. If it's a ball, you're gonna that fastball next. Get over this notion that you can catch up with that high fastball. You can't right now, and you can't hit that slider away."

"I got a hit off a breaking ball tonight." he says.

"If you could call it that. You just got lucky."

I go over it a few times. It's really simple. Pitchers always make occasional mistakes, with the possible exception of Greg Maddux a few years back.

"What happened to you and your girlfriend back in Haldeman? Her name's Disney, right?"

"Disney McLeod," Ryne says. "She's about five miles away right now. Five miles away in space."

"Go on."

"Well, thanks to you, I didn't get busted for pot or anything else," he says. "When you told me, I thought you had some other motive. You know, you were trying to scare me straight or something, but, on the other hand, what you said was a little spooky, like something out of a movie, and I got a little superstitious about it. Plus, I told Disney about it. That was a mistake."

"So, she didn't go to Carolina. She ran off with you when you signed. You broke up. She's still out here."

The beer is starting to talk. Ryne's getting a bit emotional.

"We were gangstas on the way out here," he says. "Stoned all the way. I had the deal of being on the 40-man roster, so I didn't get tested. See, I didn't use to be this way. Disney is a high-society party girl. She got hold of me and wore me out," he says.

"The sex was good."

"Unbelievable, especially on account of it being all the sex I know. She ruled me, man. She got me on the gas. She won a beauty pageant, man. Before the talent competition, she texted me, and I met her at the loading dock of the auditorium, and we split a blunt. She chewed some gum, brushed her teeth, gargled, probably, and went out and knocked 'em dead. Me and her, man, we couldn't go wrong."

"But I take it you did," I say. I'm mainly listening and trying not to act surprised at anything, which isn't much of an act. I saw a good bit of this movie myself. I gather the latest surreptitious word for marijuana/cannabis/grass/pot/weed/green/gouge, etc., is "gas."

"I rented a condo on the beach, paid up for the rest of the season," Ryne says. "When I joined the team, I was just two weeks out from playing back home. I was still awful. They didn't play me for a week. The first weekend series I was in, I went oh-for-12, batting fifth. I never got booed before.

"Meanwhile, Disney is just partying nonstop while I'm playing ball. She's hanging out with a bad crowd, a bunch of hoodlums that are like her, too young to go drinking in the bars. The weed was one thing, but she started snorting coke and God knows what else. It pissed her off that I wouldn't do it with her. I moved out. Long story short, that's why I'm rooming with a Mormon."

"That's the second baseman, isn't it? Ross West, right?"

"How'd you know?" Ryne asks.

"He's got a name that sounds like a Mormon," I say. "He's got an upright, formal kind of batting stance that reminds me of Steve Garvey or Michael Young. I think he might make a decent utility infielder in the show."

"I hope you're right. He's a really nice guy. He wants me to read the Book of Mormon."

"I never read any of it," I say. "I had a manager one time told me it should be named *Jesus: The Western.*"

"That's good. I wouldn't know. I ain't read none of it. Just told Ross I did."

"There'll be a pop quiz, kid," I say. "You know that.

"So Disney's got that big-ass Toyota truck of your'n. She's costing you a bundle. You're living in a studio apartment with a Mormon infielder. I take it the car outside is a rental."

"Yep, but me and Ross are living in the Homewood Suites."

"Not bad," I say. "I know my way around 'em."

We start talking about what has changed and what hasn't about being an up-and-coming ballplayer. He asks me if I ever smoked pot, and I told him quite a bit. During the last half of my career, it was about the least a ballplayer could do and still be popular among his mates. If I'd gotten on steroids and other performance-enhancing chemicals, I might have had a Hall of Fame career and be blackballed from getting in it. I tell him I gave up weed when I started coaching, mainly because alcohol was accepted and cannabis wasn't in my new line of work.

"I didn't find Jesus or anything, at least not in any formal sense," I say. "Mainly, I just got old."

Ah, the truth comes out.

At about 4 a.m., with a Joel McCrea western on TV, I'm thinking this athletic young man might lead me to make another dangerous walk down the street to the yonta-sack store – the guy behind the counter always ask if you "wanna sack" regardless of whether it's a stick of gum or three cans of dog food, a jar of mayonnaise, a loaf of bread, and a pack of boiled ham – for some more of that ice-cold Shiner Bock, but, now about to sob, Ryne gets around to the ulterior motive behind his summons.

Yes, he wants out of the Houston organization, and they're already tired of him after two months of mutual frustration, but they've got a lot of money tied up in him, and they'd like to find a way to unload him. He's fired his shyster agent, who took another wad of his cash with him. He wants to leave Disney McLeod in the Corpus condo, and she can have the damned Toyota monster with the knobby tires.

"I'll give you ten grand," he says. "I'll play in Class A, rookie league, instructional, wherever the Loggers want to send me. I'll behave."

It occurs to me that he's drunk right now. I am, too.

Ryne has *one more little problem.*

The truck. He signed it over to his girlfriend when he got angrier at her than he should have. Then she ran out of the considerable amount of money he gave her and didn't tell him about it. She took out a title loan on the damned thing, and he didn't know about it until she called him and said it had been repossessed. He spent half that very day essentially raising the money to pay for the truck again.

"It's just sitting in the repo lot," Ryne says. "I got the paperwork with me. I need you to go pick it up. Take a cab, an Uber, or a Lyft. Pick it up. Drive it to the condo and park it in the garage. Leave the keys. Take another cab back here."

This Uber, this Lyft, I know nothing of them. I'll try for the cab first. Why, though, is there a need for me to do this favor?

"Underneath the cover, there's a toolbox built into the bed."

"Mine's got one," I say.

"I bet yours doesn't have several vacuum-packed bags of weed in it," Ryan says.

"Can't say that it does."

"The truck is just sitting there, according to the guy I talked to," he says. "Haven't cleaned it up. Guy says it'll be shipped out on Monday or Tuesday. He says I can still pick it up if I'm there before noon."

"Noon today?"

"They close at noon on Saturday," Ryne says.

"What if I hadn't come down?"

"Believe it or not, I think I could've gotten Ross to go get it. He's a real nice fellow."

"Why don't you still do that?"

"Well, I'd really hate for him to know any details. And I'd probably have to sell my soul to the Mormon God, I reckon."

We both know I'm going to do it. I ask him what's to keep me from being arrested. He says everything will be cool. I tell him I don't want his money. If everything works out, the big club will make it worth my while. I tell him I'll accept expense money. He reaches in his overnight bag and hands me the ten grand in a manila envelope, along with the paperwork. I tell him I'll bring back the change.

At this point, I go to bed, and he's about spent, too. As I start to drift away, it occurs to me that I still haven't given him a definite yes. I'm living dangerously with a ballplayer who may or may not have had some long-term sense knocked into him, and his former girlfriend the junkie.

What a tangled web I've weaved, or at least stumbled into. Apparently, women make a fool out of me whether I know them or not, and I've got a little too much taste for danger. I didn't think the kids nowadays were as wild as in my day. I'm wrong.

CHAPTER 24
Much Ado About Nothing

Everything is a long way in Texas. Texans think nothing of driving three hours. I'm riding in the back seat of a big, long Chevrolet sedan thinking about how little sense all this makes. A conspiracy has gotten me into this mess. I reckon I'm doing it because I believe Ryne Standback really does have some gratitude for me getting him out of the last batch of trouble he was in when his little Cruella DeVille bitch's big-thinking mama tried to screw him for life. What is her name? The daughter is named Disney. I couldn't forget that. Drema, I think. I'm satisfied she's got a lot to do with her daughter's conniving ways. Disney's not a bad girl. She just loves sex and drugs, I reckon.

I owe Frank Staley Jr. He knows it. The club must really want to sign Ryne. Frank Jr., for no good reason, still wants my blessings. God loves him for that. He probably knows more about this caper than he lets on. Ryne hasn't enough guile to set me up. Frank Jr. will look out for me. Within the Portland organization, he's about the only one who thinks I know what I'm doing anymore.

Anyway, if Frank Jr. says go, I go. The only way he'd send me to prison is if there's a top-notch player there.

I can't believe a repo lot serving the considerable city of Corpus Christi is a 90-minute drive away, but it is. It's a little over halfway between Corpus and Brownsville. I expect Ryne was banking on me turning down the money he offered. It will take most than ten grand to pay for the truck and the ride to it.

With time to kill, I decide to call Taiquon's grandma. She has moved from Vosbrinck to Bluefield, the closest place with city lights, at least the kind that glitter. She doesn't answer but calls right back. My cell has an Oregon area code, and I won't get a new number because I don't want to punch in all the numbers in my contact list. A man can't look up Wade Boggs in the phone book.

"This Mister Kinlaw?"

"Clyde to you, Ophelia."

"How my grandboy doing, Mister Clyde?"

"Better than you and me both imagined," I say.

I don't much care for "Mister Clyde," but it's better than "Mister Kinlaw." It makes me feel old even though I am.

"Is he still with that girl?" she asks.

"Best I can tell. Have you not talked with him?"

"Yes, but I like to match up what he says with what you say."

"I'm not with the Bucks at the moment, Ophelia. The big-league club sent me a little troubleshooting assignment. I expect to drive back up there tomorrow."

"You're supposed to be taking care of my boy," she said.

"I am. The Portland Loggers are the reason I'm with Taiquon. They found him a place to play. They went by my suggestions. It ain't costing 'em much, not yet, but they got money invested in Taiquon and me both. My friend in the front office is looking at a trade, so he asked me to go to Corpus Christi to check out a first baseman. That's where I'm at now."

"I was gonna call you anyway," Ophelia said. "I talked to Taiquon yesterday. He didn't sound like he was exactly right in the head."

"What's that mean?"

"Oh, he just sounded like it he might've been drinking a little. I think he was on something."

"Well, he is hanging around with ballplayers," I said. "Ain't none of 'em flipped a coin between playing ball and going to the seminary. I'm a mite bit suspicious, too, but I ain't been seeing much of him except at the ballpark and on the bus. He's popular among his teammates. He's got him a girl. He's really come out of his shell since we got to Texas. I expect that's mostly a good thing."

"I hope you're right,' she said.

"You've raised him well, Ophelia. That's all you'n do. You can't live their lives for 'em."

"I want you to keep him straight, Mr. Clyde."

"If I told him what to do, it'd be a sure thing he'd do the opposite. You know the way young'uns are. I made that mistake too many times with my own. I'm damned if I'm gonna make it again with Taiquon. I'm there for him. When he asks my opinion, I give it to him, but he's got a mind of his own. I didn't see much of that in Vosbrinck. He's developing as a ballplayer just fine. He's got a lot more confidence in himself. That's bound to spill over when he steps off the diamond. You told me you trusted me when I brought him out here. You just got to trust me now. Him, too. He's a good boy. That head on his shoulders is straighter most ways than when I first got to know him."

"This little gal, this Juanita, is she all right?"

"You know her brother plays shortstop for the Bucks, right?"

"Why, yes."

"I've gotten to know her mother," I say.

"Is you seeing her?"

"No, ma'am. She's a waitress at the diner where I take my meals. Sweet woman," I say, "somethin' 'bout like you, Miss Ophelia."

"She's trouble, then," Ophelia says, chuckling.

"I'll call you again when I get back to Buckhead," I say. "Bye, now."

I can't remember what the cab driver looks like, and all I've seen is the back of his head since I told him where I was going.

As long as it is, I'm surprised he hasn't offered me financing. What little he has spoken has been Spanish, communicating with the home office. I've been in baseball long enough that I've got a fair version of broken Spanish in my bag of tricks. He hasn't been plotting my assassination unless I'm going to get it while he's having the oil changed.

Meanwhile, I'm thinking this through, a little nervous as I'm accustomed to pickup trucks but not ones with bags of contraband in them. I take some comfort in knowing this isn't a TV show. The type of fellow whose job is cleaning out a repossessed Toyota is not the type who would call the cops. He's more the type who would confiscate it for himself. Ryne says it hasn't been touched since they towed it in. I wonder how he knows that. Maybe he's setting Disney up. Wouldn't that be an interesting way to get her out of his way? I doubt that, though. She might be an obstacle in his path, but the kid would still have to be pretty cold-blooded to set up a gal who's been screwing his brains out.

None of my business. I'm just a ball scout. I keep my envelope of cash down so that the driver can't see me. I fold a few benjamins and stuff them in the pouch of my Jernigan College hoodie (undoubtedly a popular item in these parts). I can thus pay the cabbie without looking like the drug mule I might be. The possession of only hundred-dollar bills makes a generous tip likely.

I tell the cabbie, "Keep it. Buy your woman something nice."

This is something I've always wanted to say. He says, "Si, senor," which is something I've always wanted to hear.

I don't know. I don't care. I don't want to know what's in that built-in toolbox. I want to leave this play-toy truck in the parking garage at 2357 Whale's Tail Drive, with the key on top of the left-front tire, walk up the street to the playground at the municipal park, and hail another cab. Everything is going fine, but I could still drink a beer. I'm a mite jittery.

How I got to this place, I can't say. That I've been uprooted from my job to drive to the coast of Texas to be a low-level drug mule seems incomprehensible. I reckon I'm at best Frank Staley Jr.'s troubleshooter and at worst his enforcer. A deal for Standback must be imminent. It's got to be. I'm in Junior's good graces; he's the only one in Portland I've got on my side.

No cloak. No dagger. I park the truck, which I first saw in the parking lot of a sports bar in Haldeman.

CHAPTER 25

The Plot Further Thickens

I have little else to do. I'm not of a mind to head back to Buckhead just yet. I need to get back to Taiquon, but I don't feel up to it. I walk up to the office to make sure I'm paid up for another night, get the card recoded, and go back to the room to try to wash my mind of its contradictions by taking a nap. No dice. I can't help but ruminate about the myriad reasons why the hell I'm here.

Somehow, I kill a lot of time thinking. Maybe I doze off a few times so lightly that I don't realize it. It occurs to me that I pretend not to care about the decline of my baseball career. I acted like I was happy when really I was glum, numb, and bummed. A man who's been competing all his life can't quit. Taiquon Wattson lit a fire under me, and he's going to be appreciative for no good reason. Helping him hasn't got much to do with it. I'm making him a ballplayer for purely selfish reasons. I'm going to prove my detractors wrong, which is why I've let my last professional friend, Frank Staley Jr., turn me into a double-naught spy.

Yet still, it doesn't make complete sense. The plot has holes in it. Frank Jr. tells me to give Ryne Standback one more look, even though the Loggers didn't draft him. They still want to acquire him. Frank Jr. wants me to approve a kid I disapprove of. He's not doing well. He's a bargain if he's not a hopeless screw-up. The club wants him checked out. Why in the name of Hensley Meulens do they send me? What's Junior want? A come to Jesus? Repentance? Is he waiting to see if Standback can change my mind? It's a damn strange way to do it. Or does he not even know the web of intrigue into which I have stumbled?

162

In the cinematic words of Slim Pickens, "I am depressed." Not clinically depressed. Depressed for a damn good reason.

I trust Frank Jr. I've known him all his life. I'm willing to do what it takes to prove I know what I'm doing.

The strangest development of all is that I *have* changed my mind. What is it with me?

Naturally, with nothing else to do, I go back to Whataburger Field after stopping at a Whataburger for a burger. Undoubtedly, they're available in the field. I'm not thinking clearly. I pay my way in again. I don't want anyone to see me, which is a long shot in a place populated by several thousand people. Fortunately, the great majority of people who recognize me now can't quite remember my name, and if I stop in the gift shop and buy the stupidest hat available, preferably a floppy one, which I do, they think, *nah, couldn't be.* I'm just a goofy fellow who looks like Clyde Kinlaw.

It's not foolproof, but it's worth trying. What's the worst that can happen? I act slightly like an asshole, and someone says so on Twitter. I got one because the Loggers set one up in my name. If it ever forgets my password, I'll never be able to get back on. I can't remember the last time I tweeted. I show an elderly man my ticket stub, and he starts to lead me down the aisle to wipe off my seat, but I tell him I can find my way and slip him a five.

Standback's at first base, of course. He's batting eighth, which is not the preferred slot for a switch-hitting first baseman. He records a putout on a grounder to short in the top of the first, sharing the spotlight with a popup and a fly ball. My cell rings. I look at it. Frank Jr. Thank God.

I ask what's up, and Junior hears the sound of the ballpark.

"Oh, thank God," he says. "You still in Corpus Christi?"

"Well, I'm not at the World Cup finals," I say.

"I figured you'd be grumpy. Your sense of humor is better when you're pissed off."

"I reckon I got that going for me."

"Can the kid be saved?" Junior asked.

"Which one?"

"Standback," Junior says, "but, by the way, Taiquon was 4-for-4 with a bomb and two doubles last night."

He knows he must indulge my affection for the Wattson kid. Back to business.

"No, seriously, Frank, what's the deal?"

"Deal? What deal?"

"Shit," I say, a little too loudly when the crowd goes quiet. Someone for the home team struck out. I look up. It's Standback, of course. "There's always a deal."

Frank Jr. chuckles, a bit artificially for my taste.

"What do you think of Standback now?" he asks.

"Hold on a minute." I got some earbuds somewhere. I find them in that little mini-pocket above the main one in a pair of jeans. "There. Now I can hear you better and I don't feel like I have to talk so loud.

"He's learned a few lessons about life," I say. "His gal's done took him for a ride, and lately they the kind he doesn't like no more."

"That was very tactful, Clyde."

"Don't take that the wrong way. I do not mean I think he is a switch-hitter in more ways than the obvious. I mean Ryne has regained more than a semblance of humility. Oddly, I think he's off the weed precisely because his girlfriend's got on it bad."

"And he told you all this freely?" Junior asks.

"A few beers helped," I say.

"No drinking problem?"

"Nah. That was my doing. I did him a favor back home. I didn't like him, but I didn't want him ruined. Turns out, it was the right thing. He's still got quite possibly the best swing ever connected to total stupidity."

"You don't reckon you can help him with that?"

"Shit."

"I'm serious," Junior said. "What if you picked up Standback in the morning and took him back to Buckhead with you? Could you straighten him out?"

"If I can, I'm damn sure the only one."

"That's what I think, too."

"How is this even legal?" I ask.

"It takes a bit of finagling. The Bucks are not an amateur team. I can arrange Standback's unconditional release by Houston. I can take some guaranteed money off their hands. I've figured out a way to slip it through."

"Finagling" was one of his daddy's words.

"This is a deal that sounds like one your old man would make," I say.

"Thanks, Clyde. Thanks a lot. Gotta get to work on a few paperwork items."

Frank Jr. hangs up quickly, sort of like his eyes were welling up. Nah. Couldn't be. He's a grown man.

Standback plays two more innings in the field and doesn't bat again. Corpus Christi takes him out of the game. Frank Staley Jr. doesn't play.

I still can't figure out exactly how the pieces in the puzzle fit. This is bigger than a spoiled brat and a diamond in the rough. Things are turning backward and inside out. My first wife might be able to figure this out. It's one of two things she was good at.

CHAPTER 26

In It for the Ride

Between us, Ryne Standback and I can't put together a coherent story of what is going on. Ryne is happy to get out of Corpus Christi and away from Disney McLeod. I'm happy to get back to Taiquon Wattson but stimulated a bit by trying to straighten Ryne out. What the hell else have I got to do? Over the years, I've seen quite enough hell at home to develop an affinity for the road.

Ryne mainly plays with his cell, trying to stay occupied. I stop for gas and Ryne asks me if I want anything. I say I'm fine, but he returns from inside the truck plaza with two gigantic slushes – calling them smoothies apparently increases the market value – and asks me if I'd rather give myself headaches with strawberry-banana or blackberry-melon. He doesn't phrase it that way. I go with the latter because I could use a slice of watermelon. It's been a while. It's tasty, all right.

I sip, but nature calls before long. I pull off the exit at another truck plaza.

"It's important to drink lots of fluid," I say, regretting that I take a diuretic every morning. "A man can relieve the boredom of travel with frequent pissing."

"Heck, yeah," Ryne says.

He returns with another smoothie. Thankfully, he doesn't buy me one this time. Too obvious, I suppose. Ryne listens to music, I assume, on his earbuds. I tune the radio. Texas still has unique local radio stations, and not the in-and-out, bluegrass-themed AM stations of Kentucky, Virginia, and North Carolina. The

South Carolina locals generally specialize in the aging devotees of "beach music" who still dance the night away. Texas has the same mass-market stations as every other part of the country, but there are still a few powerful FM outposts that play country music unique to Texas. I'm grooving on Jerry Jeff Walker and the Gonzo Compadres when Ryne allows as to how he's got to piss again.

When we get back on the interstate, I say, "You partial to them smoothies, ain't you?"

"Good for you," he replies.

"I got a question?"

"Yeah?"

"I don't suppose you got one of them Juuls stashed away in your shirt pocket?"

I glance over and his expression says yes.

"Relax," I say. "You can stay off that weed by keeping your mind occupied. Craving that nic's tough. You don't have to hide it, and besides, if you'll just hit that thing in here, the rest of the trip'll be an hour shorter."

"It doesn't have much smell," he says.

"Weed is not physically addictive," I say. "It's psychologically addictive. Folks hit weed 'cause they love the hell out of it."

"I reckon you're right about that."

"I think about it a lot. We know a lot more about what's bad for you, but the Hall of Fame's full of players that smoked when they were out of view."

"You smoked when you played?"

"Not a lot. I think tobacco goes with booze and weed. But I've struck out three times in a game and come back to the dugout wanting to bust a cooler or something, and instead of having a fit, I'd just go down in the walkway and take a couple of quick drags on a Marlboro to settle my ass down. From what I hear, ever how bad that vaping is, it ain't as bad as cigarettes."

"You want to hit it?"

"Nah," I say, "I've gotten right partial to not having as many vices no more."

"Ain't much you haven't seen, is there?" Ryne asks.

"I reckon I've learned a little," I reply.

I can't smell the vapor. Ryne obligingly cracks the window when he lets a cloud out.

"I'm not Perry Mason," I say. "When the Loggers asked me to check you out, I didn't just watch you on the field."

It occurs to me that Ryne has no idea who Perry Mason is. He probably thinks he was a lefthanded reliever for the Kansas City A's. Except he doesn't know who they were, either.

"After a game, you and your gang came into a little bar and grill where I was already, having a burger and a beer. I left, but I waited outside, sitting in this truck."

"And you have seen me and Disney and Ben Schwartz and Beverly Dalton smoking a blunt in the parking lot."

"Yep. And chasing it with Juuls. I didn't know what they were, at first."

"How about Disney's mom? How'd you know she was out to get me?"

"She told me so," I say. "She wanted me to help."

"How much?"

"I got the slight impression I could've had her."

"And you didn't?"

"I got more sense than that," I say. "Life's too short for that woman. Good-looking, though."

Ryne gets quiet, taking it all in.

"She's really not a bad gal," he says. "She just wanted so badly to get away from her mother. When we got to Texas, Disney went wild. I couldn't do nothin' with her. I was on the road half the time. I knew I couldn't hang with that beach crowd."

"So you gave her your truck, got me to save her weed, and now, she's on her own."

"I'll try to help her when I got the time. Right now I just got to get away."

"A kid like you can get in a heap of trouble 'cause he finds a gal who spreads her legs right regularly," I say.

About that time, Johnny Bush commenced singing "If You're Gonna Do Me Wrong, Do It Right." I think Ryne might have actually listened to it.

I tell him about the Buckhead Bucks and the border league. I say I had to find a place to develop Taiquon and hide him away until he was ready for pro ball.

"To tell you the truth, I really didn't know he was that good," Ryne says.

"You were too busy watching people watching you," I say.

"You're probably right," he says, sounding older than his years.

We roll through Dallas at about nine, and the traffic isn't half bad. I tell Ryne about the lakefront cabin, converted into a duplex by Dreighton Parker to house his ringers. I tell him there are two beds in Taiquon's room.

"I wouldn't worry about privacy," I say. "Taiquon's got him a girlfriend and a car Parker let him have."

I say when Parker finds the gift I'm bringing, he's liable to give Ryne a car, too.

"I reckon I ain't gonna be here that long," he says. "I reckon I'll just catch rides with you, Clyde."

It's the best news I've heard in a while. I don't want Ryne spending too much time at the cabin with the pot-smoking pitchers, Paul Hughic and Gleason Tolson, splitting the place.

It occurs to me that I've got to give Ryne a new identity. If the P.A. announcer introduces the first baseman, Ryne Standback, several people are going to recognize his name as the first-round draft pick of a Texas major league team. I don't think it ought to be common knowledge that the new first baseman, or designated hitter since I remember the surly presence of Junior Sisler, signed for three million dollars, some of which he might still have.

"Pick a name," I say. "Any name."

He thinks for a while. "How 'bout Jack Trouble?"

"Too true," I say. "You don't want a name that draws attention. That's a big star's name right there, either that or a male stripper. A pro wrestler, maybe. You need a utility infielder's name, something like, uh, Put Jackson."

Ryne has chuckled a few times. This draws his first giggle.

"Put Jackson it is," he says.

CHAPTER 27

Calla-GOO-la

*J*half expect a party of some sort to be twisting the night away when Ryne Standback's new alter ego and I arrive back at the cabin about half past midnight. The stoners' firm of Hughie and Tolson must have both twirled in Wichita Falls, staggered home, and crashed. Taiquon's Grand Am is nowhere to be seen. Whatever he did on the diamond didn't exhaust him.

"I don't believe you need to worry about having to share a bedroom," I say to Ryne, a.k.a. "Put."

"Has he got enough sense to make sure he doesn't get her pregnant?"

"He did four nights ago," says I.

"Not that I'm a paragon of virtue," Ryne says.

"But you do know the meaning of the word 'paragon'," I say, signifying nothing.

We're both tired. It's been a whirlwind tour. It's always mystified me why driving is so tiring. I just sit on my ass and guide my truck. It's not like I walked from Corpus Christi to Buckhead. I reckon it's the concentration that driving requires, but I've been conscious of such concentration only when I've had too much to drink, and that has grown infrequent as I've gotten older.

I can't sleep late, either, which is where strong coffee comes in. I get my ass out of the rack with the requisite grunting that awakening at my age, with my knees, entails. In deference to my newer roomie, I enjoy my morning constitutional, which the dictionary says can be a walk but in my case is a movement of

171

regularity. Then I shower with the window open, which is an efficient way to remove the unpleasant aroma. Then I put on my underwear and wrap myself in a robe and rouse Ryne. While he is making himself presentable, I brew myself a mug of coffee and read my cell. When Ryne arrives, he sips his coffee and sucks his Juul, and then we head off to Clyde's because it is one of those places where a man can still get decent grits and I can at least reacquaint myself with Rosie, who might be able to shed some light on the whereabouts of her daughter and Taiquon.

Damned if the two of them aren't there, so I reintroduce the two former Palmetto State competitors, and I let the three kids mingle while I sit on a stool at the counter and engage in delightful small talk with Rosie about where I've been and why I've got yet another crazy kid with me. My time here is coming to an end soon, and we both realize it, and it fairly ruins the possibility of future intimacy. Women make a fool out of me, anyway, just like the late, great Jimmie Rodgers, "the Singing Brakeman." The conversation is quite pleasant because there is no pressure and Rosie needs another man about as much as I need another woman.

Ryne and I leave the teenagers in the heat to go over to the field where I need to see Charlie Gabbard and Ryne needs a uniform. I've never been to the clubhouse earlier than when the old equipment manager, Clarence Peebles, got there. I give him the directions and tell him he can't miss Mr. Peebles and just tell him I sent him. I head up the hall the opposite way to Charlie's office, where he and Antwine Renfro are in a high dudgeon. Something of which I am dreadfully unaware has gone amiss.

Charlie tells me that the team's second-best hitter and first-best baseman, Jeremiah "Junior" Sisler, has been busted overnight for trafficking in drugs. He says Dreighton is off right now bailing him out of jail.

"It'll be all right," I say.

"How do you figure that? We're in first place, but they're six games left to play."

"We'll be fine," I say, and I'm not hiding a smile well at all.

"Dray can get him out of jail, Clyde, but he can't play no more. It's gonna be in the paper. It's on the county website."

"The county website? I'll be dogged."

"This is serious."

"Is Junior still gon' run the concessions?" I ask.

"That's what got him in the trouble he's in," Charlie says.

"Hang on just a minute," I say. "I'll be right back."

I fetch Ryne, bring him back to the office in a road uniform he is trying on, and say, "Charlie. Antwine. This here's Ryne Standback. He was recently the first-round draft choice of Houston, and he is now the short-term property of the Buckhead Bucks because I have fetched him to fill, as pure luck would have it, the club's needs."

"Are you on something, Clyde?" Antwine asks.

"I wish," I say. "Secretly, my new friend, Mr. Standback, has been released by both the parent club and the Corpus Christi Hooks, and the paper is being pushed sufficiently slow that I can work with him and Taiquon both for the rest of the season here."

Thus am I a hero among my peers again.

"Reckon you old boys can keep a secret?" I ask.

They are too stunned to speak.

"We don't want his name on no roster," I say. "Ryne and I have jointly decided his Buckhead Bucks name is Put Jackson. Let me think of a hometown that is just as good. Put – tell the P.A. announcer that his name is Putnam – hails from ... Caligula, Missouri. They's no such place, of course, but tell the microphone man it's pronounced 'Cal-uh-GOO-luh.' That'll work just fine, if I do say so myself."

Damned if everybody ain't in a good mood now.

"How can you pull this off?" Charlie asks.

"I can't. I know somebody in the Loggers front office who can, though. I don't know how. I don't want to know how. I reckon you understand the importance of my absence now."

"Damndest thing ever I seen," Charlie says, "but I'll kiss you on the mouth if you want me to."

"I'll pass," I reply.

In the hot sun, I put a wooden stool next to the mound so that I can adequately hydrate as I toss batting practice to "Put" and intersperse it with yelled instructions that echo through the empty yard. I ask him if ever in his life he has hit the ball intentionally to the opposite field.

"I can't do nothing but pull lefthanded," Put says. "I'm natural-born righthanded, and I can hit it the opposite way on that side."

"Show me," I say. "Turn around."

I throw a series of lollipop curves on the outside of the plate, and when he takes the first one I throw out of the park to left-center field, I am unimpressed.

"Opposite field," I say. "Hit it where it's pitched. Slap an outside pitch to right."

He gradually gets better. He gradually starts bathing in sweat.

"I brought some water out here with me," I say. "Want some?"

I remember being taught that a man ought not to drink ice water that fast lest he keel over dead with heatstroke, but this Put Jackson, he's a well-conditioned athlete, and he only needs two more water breaks while I try with modest success to teach him how to hit the opposite way from the left side. He works hard, but I don't want to wear him out because he's got a bus trip and a game tonight in Ada, Oklahoma. I get him to lug the cooler, which isn't much of a lug since much of the water has been imbibed by the two of us, while I carry the stool back to the dugout. While we're sitting there, and I'm trying to see if he's got a brain in his head, he pulls his Juul out of the back pocket of his uniform pants and starts hitting it every so often. Somehow, that store-bought, beautiful, uppercut swing has never been used to adapt to outside pitching. His agent probably had it written into his contract.

Put's going to fit in with this bunch just fine.

I consider driving up into Oklahoma with my truck and talk hitting with "Put," but I decide I need to spend some time with Taiquon, so I slide in next to him on the bus and let Put get to know his teammates. Taiquon is either fine or he's gotten better still at conning my ass. I shouldn't think the worst of the kid, but he is unfortunately hindered by the memory of how I reacted when I first learned how to experience the reliable availability of a tight space to spend the best part of my nights. He is enjoying the Garden of Eden and picking every single forbidden fruit off the vine. A stern lecture only succeeds in inspiring a strapping young lad to enjoy the fruit double. I wish he'd ask a few questions, but in an astonishingly short time, Taiquon has learned plenty enough to be dangerous. He's a good enough kid to believe it's love but bad enough not to pass judgment on whether or not lust is the same thing. Truly is he walking through the gates of manhood? As I told his grandmother recently in as many words, there's as much good as bad in that. At a thirty-five-year distance, I miss that jiggy feeling myself.

Taiquon does inform me proudly that his batting average has risen to .456, which, he says, leads the Border League by 102 points. Two months ago, he probably didn't know how to figure a batting average out.

I tell young Putnam Jackson to get his rest at the yard, since he didn't get any on the bus ride up. Of course, he takes batting practice and doesn't look particularly good since, following my directions, he concentrates on hitting the opposite field. Charlie is impressed enough, anyway, to place him fourth in the lineup, right behind Taiquon in the place previously occupied by Junior Sisler.

In the top of the first inning, Jesus Garcia strikes out. Josh Mizell hits a popup that the Ada catcher handles near the screen on the third-base size. Taiquon steps up to the plate. I step out of the dugout and kneel next to Put in the on-deck circle.

"If Taiquon gets on, you're going to have a rare opportunity," I say.

"Why you say that?" Minor league baseball has thus far taught him the art of wiping his bat with gobs of pine tar.

"That little sawed-off righty knows nothing about you, uh, Put. That means there is a high priority he will groove you a mediocre fastball – it's that at best – right down the middle of the plate. I'd say there's a ninety percent chance that's what he's gonna throw. He figures you're the newbie, and you'll likely take the first pitch. What he doesn't know is I'm sitting right here telling you to sit on that pitch and if it ain't a slider or fastball eyeball-high, knock the piss out of it."

"I always take a strike," Put says.

"Not no more. And you have my permission to pull it."

Taiquon singles up the middle. I walk back to the dugout.

"What'd you tell him?" Charlie asks.

"You'll see."

The Man from Caligoola – I had spelled and pronounced it for the announcer during batting practice in the off chance that he'd otherwise say Put was from a town named after a depraved Roman emperor – steps into the box. He hits that first piece of cheese about as far as anyone in this burg has ever seen. I reckon he hit it about 450 feet. The Chickasaws' sprinkling of fans – Ada, I learned from my new friend the P.A. announcer in the home-team player introductions, is the headquarters of the Chickasaw Nation – probably called it 500 feet by the next morning and 600 by the end of the week and immediately went into the same shock as the would-be Native Americans themselves, who quickly gave up five more two-out runs to trail 7-0 before they batted.

"Just add water" is what I always say.

EPILOGUE

*J*didn't understand the reason for Frank Staley Jr.'s actions for quite some time. I reckon you could say my obedience was unconditional. He was the only ally in the Loggers organization I had left, the only one who listened to what I had to say and put some stock in it.

Thanks to two athletes different in almost every way – one a poor black kid, the other a spoiled rich brat – I got my good reputation back. I deserved some credit, too. I developed them athletically and answered their questions honestly in a thousand other ways, but neither was made of silly putty and they both had natural skills that I happened to have the right style to cultivate.

Taiquon Wattson and Ryne Standback came from both ends and met in the middle.

The Border League season ended prematurely. The Buckhead Bucks won every game but one; that was while I was away and it was 19-18 on a walk-off grand slam. The Bucks were 14-1, and the next best team, Wichita Falls, was 8-7. The playoffs were canceled for lack of interest. I left my truck at the cabin, and the three of us flew to Portland, where Frank Jr. oversaw the workout. He already had Ryne under contract, and he cut Taiquon a check for $50 grand, which, upon my recommendation, Taiquon sent $10,000 to his grandma, kept $10,000 for himself, and sent the rest to Jimmy Daggett to handle the taxes and invest what was left. I sent Jimmy a heap of money, too. Frank Jr. made it worth my while, but I had to spend another month in the hot sun of the instructional league before I got it.

My lessons were professional. Taiquon, who had successfully played dumb when I first got to know him, was smarter than Ryne ever thought about being. The arrogance of being surrounded in high school by hangers-on had the effect of dumbing him down. He didn't have a bad mind. He had just forgotten the need to use it. Ryne already had the store-bought swing; I just taught him the proper time to use it.

When all the analytics were completed, the Portland experts on left swing angle, and impact velocity – it drives me crazy when they talk about the exit speed of a ball that doesn't exit – rated Taiquon higher than Ryne. After spring practice the following year, Taiquon got sent to Double-A in Spokane, Washington, and Ryne to High-A in Bend, Oregon. As it turned out, I wasn't far away.

By the end of the season, both were listed among minor league baseball's top ten prospects. Frank Jr. got the credit from the organization, and he gave me the credit. The principal owner of the Loggers, a quirky dotcom billionaire, got over seeing the son of the former owner is some kind of threat. When Jody Bjorkssen cleaned house, he made Frank Jr. the general manager, which as what he should have been for about a decade. Frank Jr. gave me his old post as director of player development, and it actually worked out well. All the sabermetricians and algorithmics kept all the analytics and passed them up the line to me, and I broke ties by analyzing the intangibles. I looked at whether a young fireballer had the balls to be a closer or if a slugger was better or worse when it mattered.

Then it all stopped dead at just about the moment the Loggers were considering whether to bring Taiquon and/or Ryne to the bigs. Damn COVID. I was about to buy a house in the hills between Portland and the coast when I got sent back to Youngville to stay at home and be on Zoom calls. Ryne had no interest in returning to Haldeman, being as how the McLeods had wanted him in prison before he left and might kill him now. He stayed with me, and I played my guitar enough that Ryne actually seemed to enjoy it. It's more evidence that Taiquon is smarter. He and Juana now live in the house that Ophelia Sanders never got around to selling. She's found a boyfriend in Bluefield, and she's having the time of her life. It's entirely possible that Miss Ophelia might birth a young'un before Juana does. I hope so. She's a good-looking woman for her age, and Taiquon and Juana have no idea how much more money they need before they bring a child into the world. I hope they give it a year, and I think it's likely. Taiquon is still driving that white Grand Am that Dreighton Parker gave him as a parting gift.

Ryne and I watch the Loggers play in front of empty houses on late-night TV. We wear our masks to get in the door then take 'em off and have breakfast most mornings at Red's on the Square because I love grits and can't make 'em for shit.

I'd let a cowboy ride on my back if it would allow me to buck on out of this stall I'm in. Ryne's taken to running and says it gives him time to think. I ride around in the truck if I want to think. I'm either putting on weight or I've got the only leather belt in the world that contracts instead of stretches, and Ryne wants to go to the weight room. My time is in the waiting room because my doctor got me to wear something called compression socks.

I'd love to play golf with Lawyer Daggett, Vern Crosley, and Dub Whatley.

I enjoy drinking beer with Ryne during those late-night games from Portland. Usually, it's just one or two, but I like tying one on every now and again, in other words, about once or twice a week. Put beer in our bellies, and we really get good at being honest. I love to play and sing old country songs with a good beer buzz. A man'll hit notes drunk he won't try sober. Some people say I just think I'm a better singer when I'm drunk. Ryne knows that's bullshit. He'll vouch for me.

I went to Texas to make a man out of the kid I loved, and now I'm back in Youngville living with the kid I despised, and damned if he hasn't become a man, too. Even I can see the irony in that.

ABOUT THE AUTHOR

The Latter Days is Monte Dutton's ninth novel. The first two, *The Audacity of Dope* (2011) and *The Intangibles* (2013), were published by Neverland Publishing, LLC. The third, *Crazy of Natural Causes* (2015), and *Forgive Us Our Trespasses* (2016), were released in the KindleScout program. He has since published a modern western, *Cowboys Come Home* (2016); two related stock-car racing adventures, *Lightning in a Bottle* (2017) and *Life Gets Complicated* (2018); and *Don't Ask, Don't Tell* (2018, 2023).

Dutton is a graduate of Furman University who lives in Clinton, South Carolina.